The Christmas Deception Unmasking the Dark Truth of Santa

Morgan B. Blake

Published by CopyPeople.com, 2024.

Table of Contents

The Christmas Reversal

In the small, snow-covered town of Ashford, Christmas had always been a time of joy. Families gathered, children eagerly awaited their gifts, and the streets shimmered with lights that decorated every home like a glittering promise of hope. The Wilsons were no exception. They lived in a modest house at the edge of town, their little corner of the world tucked in between the dark forests that seemed to surround everything like an impenetrable wall. This year, the Wilsons had a special excitement—they had just moved in, and it would be their first Christmas in their new home.

For weeks, the children, Billy and Emma, had been counting down the days, eagerly checking the calendar and discussing their wish lists at the dinner table. The house smelled of cinnamon and pine, the air crisp with the expectation of something magical. Their father, James, had decorated the house with lights and tinsel, as he always did, trying to keep the old family traditions alive, despite the quiet whispers of concern in the town.

The town had always been a little strange—people spoke of old stories, of families who'd disappeared, of the strange coldness that seemed to settle over Ashford once the first snow fell. But James had never paid much attention to such things. He believed in Christmas, in the magic, in the joy. So when a large, heavily wrapped package appeared on their doorstep on Christmas Eve, he thought nothing of it. It was just another gift from Santa Claus.

Billy and Emma were beside themselves with excitement as they gathered around the enormous box. James smiled, watching them tear into it, oblivious to the sense of unease creeping over him. Inside, they found the most beautiful dolls and toys—too perfect, in fact, almost too beautiful to be real. Their eyes were unnaturally lifelike, their smiles too wide. But the children didn't notice. They squealed with joy, already pulling their new treasures from the box and running around the house.

That night, as James tucked his children into bed, he noticed something strange. The toys had been placed carefully on the table, but their eyes... they seemed to follow him as he moved around the room. He shook it off as a trick of the light. After all, what did he know about toys? What did anyone?

He tried to ignore the growing unease inside him as he turned off the lights and headed downstairs. There, he poured himself a drink and sank into his favorite armchair. He wanted to believe it was all just the stress of moving, the anxiety of a new home and new job. But something felt wrong. The air in the house was too still, too heavy. The silence was unnerving, as though the house itself was holding its breath.

James tried to shake the feeling, but it only deepened. He stood up and walked to the kitchen, intending to make himself a cup of tea. But as he passed the window, he froze. Outside, through the snowstorm, a shadow passed by, too large to be human. He squinted, pressing his face against the glass, but the shadow was gone before he could make sense of it. He opened the door cautiously, calling out into the storm. There was no response, only the soft whisper of the wind.

The feeling of dread was now undeniable. His children were sleeping upstairs, but the toys—they were wrong. He needed to check on them, needed to make sure everything was okay. As he walked toward the living room, he found the dolls sitting in a perfect row, their glassy eyes fixed on him. He reached out to touch one, but recoiled instantly. It was cold, unnaturally so, as if it had been sitting in ice.

Suddenly, the door slammed behind him. He turned, his heart racing, but there was no one there. The room had gone completely still, the only sound the faint rustling of the storm outside. Then he heard it—low at first, a voice coming from the corner of the room, a whisper barely audible above the howling wind.

"Santa's gift is never what it seems."

James's blood ran cold. He turned, but the room was empty, save for the dolls—who now seemed to smile wider, their faces more contorted. His hand gripped the back of the chair, knuckles white with fear.

He staggered backward toward the stairs, feeling the weight of the house pressing down on him, each step echoing unnervingly in the silence. The dolls. The strange shadow outside. Something was wrong, horribly wrong. He rushed upstairs, calling his children's names in a voice that trembled despite his best efforts.

When he reached their room, he found them sleeping soundly, unaware of the terror that had begun to envelop their home. He kissed their foreheads, but as he did, he saw something that made his heart stop—there, in the corner of the room, a figure stood, its outline barely visible against the moonlight.

Santa Claus.

But this was not the jolly man James remembered from his childhood. The figure in the corner was twisted, its face pale and gaunt, its eyes dark pits of emptiness. Its red suit was stained, and the once-friendly beard was matted and dirty. The air grew colder, and James felt his breath catch in his throat as the figure stepped forward, its movements unnaturally slow, deliberate.

"It's too late," it said, its voice a hollow, bone-chilling whisper. "Your disbelief is your undoing."

James's mind raced as the realization hit him—Santa was not who he thought he was. This was not the man who brought joy, but Satan himself, in disguise, feeding on the souls of those who believed too strongly in his false image. The toys. The coldness. The shadow outside. It had all been part of the plan, a dark magic designed to draw him in, to make him doubt everything, until there was nothing left but the truth that had always been there.

He turned to run, to escape, but as his foot hit the first step, the floorboards groaned and cracked beneath him. The house was collapsing, the walls closing in. The dolls, now fully animated, moved toward him, their eyes glowing with an unnatural light. The last thing James saw before the darkness overtook him was the twisted smile of the figure he had once trusted—Santa Claus, his true form now revealed in all its monstrous glory.

And in that final moment, the house seemed to laugh—low, menacing, as if the very walls themselves had conspired against him.

No one survives the Christmas Reversal.

For in the end, the belief that one is safe is the greatest lie of all.

Coal in the Furnace

Every year, when December rolled around, Emma thought of Christmas with a bitter kind of resignation. Her childhood had been filled with holiday cheer, sure, but those days had long passed. As an adult, the season had become nothing more than a reminder of the emptiness she had come to feel about the world and herself. There were no more stockings hung by the chimney, no more lights twinkling in the windows, no more anticipation of presents from a mysterious man in a red suit.

Christmas was now just a series of days to get through—work deadlines, family obligations, and endless shopping. But then, one cold December evening, she received an envelope that seemed too significant to ignore. The handwriting on the front was unfamiliar, elegant, yet hurried. Inside, a single card with a crude, hand-drawn image of a chimney and a pile of coal. Beneath it, the message was simple: "You've been naughty. Come to the Furnace."

It unsettled her, of course. She'd been in a dark place lately, but she had never been one to believe in superstition or ghost stories. Yet something about the card felt... wrong. The kind of wrong that prickled at the back of her neck.

She dismissed it at first. But the card continued to gnaw at her, the words becoming more like an obsession. The Furnace. What did it mean? Who had sent this? It wasn't until the third day after the card's arrival that she decided to look into it. She started by searching online, typing in every possible combination of the words "The Furnace," "coal," and "Christmas." Nothing but folklore about the traditional coal gift for naughty children, nothing of substance.

Then, almost as if guided by something invisible, Emma found a town—Ashford. A town known for its strange customs, dark secrets, and an unusual number of people who disappeared every Christmas. According to the obscure accounts she read, the town had a peculiar tradition: each year, someone would be burned alive, their death marked by a massive fire that consumed the central square. It had all the hallmarks of a twisted, ancient ritual. And it had happened every Christmas for over a century.

Something compelled Emma to go there, though she couldn't explain why. Ashford was far from her home, and she hadn't even told anyone where she was going. She packed a bag and drove through the icy roads that wound into the town, her heart thudding louder with each passing mile.

As she arrived, the first thing she noticed was the silence. The streets were eerily empty, the houses dark, their windows blank as if staring at her. There were no Christmas lights, no festive decorations, only a strange coldness in the air that seemed to seep into her bones. She drove past rows of houses that seemed forgotten by time, the town square ahead.

The smell of burning wood was thick in the air, and the distant glow of firelight flickered ominously against the thick black sky. As she stepped out of her car, Emma felt the oppressive weight of something ancient, something watching her, surrounding her. There, in the middle of the square, was a massive bonfire that crackled and roared with an unnatural intensity. The flames rose high, twisting and curling like snakes in the night, and yet there was no one to be seen, no crowd gathering, no voices.

Emma's skin prickled with fear, but something—some dark curiosity—drove her closer to the fire. As she stepped into the square, she heard a voice, faint and whispering through the wind. "The Furnace claims all who wander here."

Suddenly, the ground beneath her seemed to tremble. The fire crackled louder, and from the flames, a figure emerged—a tall, shadowed form draped in a tattered red cloak, its face obscured by a hood. It moved toward her with an unnatural grace, as if the fire itself had summoned it.

"Do you know why you are here?" the figure asked, its voice low and rasping.

Emma tried to speak but found her throat dry, her voice stuck in her chest. The figure continued, as if expecting her answer.

"You were given a gift," it said. "A gift you didn't understand. The coal, the card… they were warnings. Warnings that you were never meant to ignore."

Emma's heart raced, panic rising in her throat as the figure raised a hand, pointing toward the fire. In the center of the flames, something shifted. Through the flickering light, she saw faces—familiar faces—burning, their eyes wide with terror, mouths frozen in screams.

"The Furnace," the figure said again. "It consumes those who've lost their way. Those who live their lives with selfishness, who take from others and leave nothing but ashes. Every Christmas, a soul is chosen, marked by the coal they receive. It is a gift from Santa himself."

The words hit her like a punch to the gut. The coal, the warning—she had been a part of it all along, whether she realized it or not. The fire, the ritual, the deaths—it was all tied to her own life, her own choices. She had been greedy, consumed by her own bitterness, her own need for power, for control. She had always believed that she could escape the consequences of her actions, that she could keep moving through life without ever truly facing what she'd become.

But here, in this cursed town, it was clear that the past was never so easily outrun.

The figure began to move closer, its form blurring in the heat of the flames. "You've been given your final chance, Emma," it said. "The gift is yours to claim. The coal. The fire. The end of your reckoning."

Without thinking, Emma turned and ran, her breath coming in ragged gasps. She bolted back toward her car, the flames chasing her in the distance, but she knew—deep down—that it was too late. The fire would consume her. There would be no escape from the choices she had made, the path she had taken.

And just before she reached the car, she stumbled, falling to her knees. The ground seemed to crack open beneath her. The last thing she saw before everything went black was the flicker of coal, glowing in the distance.

Emma had been too late. The Furnace had claimed its final prize.

In the end, it wasn't the coal that burned the deepest, but the choices she had made long before. And as the fire consumed her, the lesson was clear: sometimes, the price of selfishness is paid not just in ashes—but in damnation itself.

Ho Ho Ho, Satan's Call

The winter wind howled through the streets of Ravenswood, rattling the old houses and whipping the fallen leaves into frenzied spirals. The Anderson family, like many others, was preparing for Christmas. But unlike the bright-eyed children in other homes, the Andersons felt a strange weight settling over them as the holiday season approached.

Catherine Anderson, a mother of two, had always loved Christmas. It had been her favorite time of the year since childhood—the scent of pine, the warmth of the fire, the joy of giving and receiving gifts. But this year, something felt different. The twinkling lights on their tree seemed to cast long, eerie shadows in the corners of the room, and the laughter of her children, Sarah and Peter, seemed too high-pitched, almost unnatural. It was as if the season had become a charade—a mask hiding something darker.

It started with the laughter. It wasn't much at first, a low, throaty chuckle that Catherine thought she had imagined. But then, as Christmas Eve drew closer, the sound became more pronounced, echoing through the halls of their home, growing louder with each passing night. It was a laugh—deep and resounding, unmistakably jolly—but there was something wrong about it. A sinister undertone that sent a chill down her spine.

At first, Catherine thought it was just her imagination playing tricks on her. But then it came again, louder this time, unmistakable—"Ho Ho Ho." The sound reverberated through the walls, as if it were coming from somewhere deep within the house. She found herself freezing in place whenever she heard it, her heart racing as the sound echoed in her ears.

"Did you hear that?" Catherine asked one evening as they sat together in the living room, the warmth of the fire flickering brightly.

Her husband, Mark, didn't seem to notice. "Hear what, hon?"

"The laughter," Catherine replied, her voice trembling.

Mark shrugged, dismissing it with a chuckle. "It's Christmas, Cat. You're just hearing things. You've been stressed with work and everything."

But Catherine wasn't convinced. She couldn't shake the feeling that something wasn't right. And it wasn't just the laughter. It was everything—the way the shadows seemed to cling to the corners of the room, the way the wind howled more fiercely around their house than it ever had before. Even Sarah and Peter seemed... different. Their eyes glimmered with a strange intensity whenever they looked at her, their voices too high-pitched, too perfect in their joy.

It wasn't until the night before Christmas that Catherine's suspicions began to take shape. As the family gathered around the tree to exchange gifts, the laughter came again. This time, it was louder, closer, and more... menacing. "Ho Ho Ho." The deep, resonant laugh echoed in their ears, causing Sarah and Peter to look toward the front door with wide, expectant eyes.

Catherine felt a cold wave wash over her. "Where is that coming from?" she whispered to herself.

Then, the doorbell rang.

Mark jumped up to answer it, but Catherine hesitated. She felt a deep sense of dread creeping through her veins as she stood frozen, staring at the door. Something was wrong. She could feel it in her bones.

Mark opened the door to reveal nothing but the snow-covered porch. There was no one there. No car parked in the driveway, no footsteps in the fresh snow. Just the cold night air. But then, as he stepped back inside, the laughter came again. Louder. More insistent. "Ho Ho Ho."

"Where's it coming from?" Mark asked, looking around, bewildered.

Catherine's gaze shifted toward the chimney. Her heart hammered in her chest. That laugh—it wasn't just Santa's laugh. It was something else. A ritualistic sound, an incantation, as if someone—or something—was trying to summon something. And then it hit her. The way the words repeated. The rhythm. The pattern.

It wasn't a festive laugh. It was a chant.

Her pulse quickened as the realization dawned on her. "It's... it's a spell."

Suddenly, the room felt colder, and the fire in the hearth dimmed. Mark, who had been looking at her in confusion, turned toward the fireplace. There, in the shifting shadows, something was moving. Something huge, dark, and formless.

"Mark, get the kids—get them out of here," Catherine cried, her voice frantic. "Now!"

Mark opened his mouth to speak, but his words were lost in a sudden wave of cold that swept through the room. The fireplace crackled with unnatural energy as the form in the shadows grew larger, taking shape. At first, it was just a dark silhouette, but then it became clearer. A figure, tall and cloaked in tattered red robes, its face obscured by a long, flowing white beard.

"No..." Catherine whispered, her voice barely audible. "It's him... Santa."

But this wasn't the jolly old man from the stories. This was something else entirely. The figure stepped forward, and as it did, the room seemed to warp around it, stretching and distorting as though reality itself was bending to its will.

"Ho Ho Ho," the figure intoned, its voice a deep, guttural rumble. "You've been naughty, Catherine Anderson. You've been doubting. And now you will pay."

Catherine stepped back, but the figure's eyes burned into her, black as the void. The laughter grew louder, filling every corner of the room, drowning out her thoughts. Sarah and Peter stood by the tree, their faces now cold and expressionless, their eyes glowing with an unholy light. They didn't move. They didn't speak.

"It's time," the figure said, its voice crackling like fire. "The sacrifice is complete."

Before Catherine could react, the room spun, and she found herself standing in a vast, desolate landscape. The house was gone. The warmth of the fire had vanished, replaced by an endless expanse of blackness, with only the distant flicker of flames in the sky. The figure loomed before her, and she realized with horror that the true meaning of Christmas was not joy, but destruction. Santa Claus had been a guise for the devil, and her family had been chosen for a ritual that had been centuries in the making.

The last thing Catherine heard before everything went dark was the voice of the figure, its laugh echoing in the cold air.

"Ho Ho Ho. You were always meant to be mine."

And with that, the flames swallowed them whole, and the Andersons became part of the underworld's eternal sacrifice. Christmas had been their final gift, and their souls were now lost forever.

The Christmas Tree Demon

The Christmas season always brought a certain excitement to the Caldwell household. The smell of pine, the twinkling lights, the promise of gifts under the tree—every year, it was a ritual of warmth and joy. For seven-year-old Olivia, it was the one time of year she could almost forget the tension that simmered between her parents, the distance between them widening with every passing year. Christmas was her escape. She could immerse herself in the lights and decorations, imagining that all was well in the world, that the dark corners of their lives could be pushed into oblivion, if only for a few days.

This year, however, something was different. It started when she was helping her father, Michael, unpack the family's Christmas ornaments. Most of them were old—passed down through generations, sentimental trinkets that had become a staple of the holiday. But there was one ornament, an odd, gnarled figure with a sharp, jagged shape, wrapped in dark red and gold thread, that caught Olivia's attention. She had never seen it before. It didn't belong with the rest of the decorations. It looked out of place—too ancient, too foreboding for the cheerful spirit of the season.

She reached for it before her father could stop her. "What's this, Dad?" she asked, her fingers brushing over the surface. It felt cold to the touch, like metal, and as she held it, she felt an unsettling pulse, faint but undeniable. It was as though the ornament was alive, aware, watching.

"Put that down, Liv," Michael said sharply. "That one's not for you to touch."

Olivia was confused. "Why not?"

Her father hesitated, eyes darting away from her for just a moment before he grunted. "It's an old family heirloom. A reminder of... things best left forgotten. Leave it be."

The warning unsettled her, but her curiosity only deepened. As the tree went up, Olivia couldn't keep her eyes off the ornament, even though it was now hanging on the highest branch, barely visible behind the shimmering lights and tinsel. It was the one thing on the tree that seemed to pulse with a dark energy, and every time she looked at it, a feeling of dread twisted in her chest. But there was something else too, something that called to her.

As Christmas Eve approached, Olivia's obsession grew. She spent hours staring at the ornament, imagining that it moved, that it somehow seemed to shift whenever she wasn't looking directly at it. She began to dream about it too—strange, disturbing dreams in which she was standing in a vast, blackened forest, the ornament hanging in front of her like a guiding star. A voice would whisper her name, beckoning her to take it down. It was in the dreams that she first heard the voice, soft at first, like a breeze rustling through dead leaves, but it was unmistakable, pulling her toward the ornament.

On Christmas morning, as Olivia tore into her gifts with the enthusiasm of a child, she noticed that her father had left her one last present, a small box wrapped in dark green paper. There was something off about it—the edges were rough, the paper uneven, as though it had been hastily thrown together. She opened it slowly, revealing a simple, black stone, smooth and cold to the touch. There was no note, no explanation. Just the stone. But the moment her fingers brushed against it, she felt something stir inside her, a dark presence that began to grow, gnawing at her insides.

That night, as the house fell silent and the world outside was blanketed in snow, Olivia could no longer resist. She crept down the stairs, the ornament beckoning her from the corner of the living room. The lights on the tree were dim now, casting long shadows across the walls. She approached the tree, her hands trembling as she reached for the gnarled ornament.

The instant her fingers made contact with it, the room seemed to shift. The lights flickered, and the air grew thick with the smell of burning pine and something else—something sour, like rotting flesh. The ground beneath her seemed to tremble, and for a brief moment, Olivia thought she saw the ornament's eyes. Eyes that were ancient, cold, and filled with malice.

Before she could pull her hand away, the tree erupted with a deafening crack. The lights exploded, sending shards of glass into the air. The temperature dropped, and in the chaos, Olivia saw it—the thing that had been bound to the ornament. It was tall, monstrous, covered in shifting shadows, with arms that stretched far too long and a face that was both human and animal, twisted with a hunger that seemed to pierce through time itself.

Olivia stumbled back, her heart pounding in her chest, but the creature was already moving toward her. Its voice filled the room, low and guttural, like the growl of a beast.

"Thank you for releasing me."

Her breath caught in her throat. "W-What are you?" she managed to whisper.

The creature chuckled, a laugh that echoed like the ringing of bells in a distant, forgotten land. "I am what you brought forth. I am the darkness that festers in every soul, the hunger that you feed with each holiday, each celebration of false joy. The ornament—your family's tree—has kept me bound for centuries. But now, I am free."

Olivia tried to scream, but her voice was swallowed by the creature's presence. It was as if the very air around her had thickened, become a part of the creature itself. The floor groaned beneath her feet, and the house seemed to come alive with the sound of cracking wood and splintering beams.

In the distance, she heard her father calling her name, but she could not look away from the thing that towered over her. The voice was no longer just a whisper—it was a roar inside her head, deafening and overwhelming.

"You think this is a time for joy?" the creature growled. "This holiday, like all holidays, is a lie. A lie you've wrapped in lights and tinsel to hide the truth. The trees, the gifts, the traditions—they are not for celebration. They are rituals, rituals that have always been meant to feed me."

And as it spoke, the creature's eyes locked onto hers, and Olivia understood. She had unknowingly unleashed something that had been lying dormant for centuries, something that had fed on the souls of those who decorated their trees, who celebrated the holidays without understanding the darkness they had summoned.

The creature reached out, its long, clawed fingers brushing her skin, and as it did, the world around her faded. The house crumbled into dust, and Olivia felt herself pulled into the void, a part of the darkness itself, lost forever.

Christmas had always been more than a holiday. It was a ritual, a pact between mankind and the forces they never understood. And with every tree they decorated, every gift they gave, they unknowingly fed the demon that had waited patiently for its freedom.

In the end, Olivia had learned the hard truth: the light of Christmas was a facade, and the tree—the tree was the vessel that brought forth destruction.

Odin's Secret

The town of Elmsford had always been a place of quiet, forgotten history. Nestled between dark forests and rolling hills, it was a town that few outside its borders knew about, and fewer still ever visited. But for those who lived there, the town held a peculiar charm. It was a place where the past was never truly buried—where stories, once whispered around hearths, still lingered in the corners of old buildings and weathered stones.

This Christmas, something was different.

Emily Bennett had grown up in Elmsford, but in recent years, she had moved away. Yet, something tugged at her as the holiday season approached. She had received a strange letter in the mail—an invitation to return home for a reunion of sorts, a "celebration of the ancient holiday customs" her family had once followed. The letter, written in elegant but slightly faded ink, was signed only with a symbol she didn't recognize—a mark of two intertwined circles.

At first, she dismissed it as some sort of family joke or a misguided attempt to rekindle a childhood tradition. But as Christmas Eve drew nearer, the sense of foreboding grew. Something was off about the letter, something that tugged at her memory, at something long buried in her childhood. Her grandmother had often spoken of "the old ways" in hushed tones, and Emily recalled vague stories of a time when the town celebrated not Christmas, but something darker, something tied to ancient rituals.

Curiosity, mingled with unease, led Emily back to Elmsford.

When she arrived, the town looked as it always had—quiet, with an old-world charm. But as she made her way through the streets, she noticed subtle changes. The usual holiday decorations had been replaced with symbols she couldn't quite place—runes carved into the sides of buildings, wreaths of holly draped over doorways, each adorned with strange sigils. The festive cheer she remembered was absent, replaced by an unsettling stillness.

Emily arrived at the old family home, where her relatives gathered around the fire, exchanging warm greetings. But the atmosphere was strange. The family members, once vibrant and full of laughter, were now distant, their eyes hollow, their smiles forced. There was an underlying tension in the air, a subtle discomfort that none of them seemed willing to acknowledge.

The head of the family, her uncle Richard, was the one who welcomed her inside. He looked tired, older than she remembered, with eyes that seemed to carry the weight of something far darker. He wasted no time in leading her into the back room, where the letter had instructed her to go.

"Emily," he began, his voice strained. "You've returned just in time for the final celebration. We've all been waiting for you."

The room was dimly lit, the air thick with the smell of incense. A large table at the center was covered in intricate carvings and strange offerings—candles, herbs, and something that looked like an ancient book.

"This..." Richard continued, pausing as if the words were heavy on his tongue, "is the final gathering. The town has been following these traditions for generations, but tonight, it's all coming to a head. We are preparing for what is to come. For the return of him."

Emily's stomach churned. "Him? What are you talking about?"

Her uncle's eyes flickered to the doorway, and then he closed the door behind her with a quiet click. "You remember the stories. The old ones. The tales of the god who once ruled the heavens, but was cast down. The one who, in his fury, took on a new form—a new name. He became the bringer of darkness, of destruction. And now, he is coming back to claim his throne."

The room seemed to close in around her. "Odin?" Emily whispered, the name slipping from her lips before she could stop herself.

Richard nodded, his face grim. "Odin. The god who was once the king of Asgard, who gave his eye for wisdom. But in time, he became something else. Something darker. His power waned as mankind moved on from the old gods, but now, with the revival of this ancient cult, his power has returned. And this night, we will offer ourselves to him, to the one who waits in the shadows."

Emily's blood ran cold. "No. This isn't right. This isn't what we—what you—believe!"

But her uncle's face was resolute. "It's too late. The rituals are already in motion. The sacrifices will be made. Christmas is the time of rebirth, yes, but not for what you think. It is the time when the veil between the worlds is thinnest. And tonight, we shall open the gate for him."

Suddenly, the ground trembled, and the house seemed to shudder as if in anticipation. The dim lights flickered, casting eerie shadows against the walls. From the corner of the room, a deep voice spoke, so low and guttural that Emily could feel it reverberating in her chest.

"Ho Ho Ho."

The voice, deep and menacing, sent a chill down her spine. It wasn't just a jolly laugh—it was a call, a summons to something ancient and terrifying. The door to the back room slammed open, and the dark figure that stepped into the room was unmistakable. A man—tall, with long silver hair and a beard that seemed to twist and writhe in the shadows. His eyes were empty, black voids that bore into her soul.

"Odin?" Emily whispered, her voice trembling.

The figure nodded, his lips curling into a cold smile. "You are the last of your line, Emily. And now, you shall serve me as your ancestors did before you."

Her heart pounded in her chest. "No! You're not—this is some sick game!"

But Odin's voice was unyielding. "There is no game, child. This is the end of your kind's false hope, the end of your civilization's petty joys. Christmas is not about light or life. It is about death. The return of the old gods. The return of darkness."

The room grew colder, and Emily felt the weight of the truth crashing over her. Her family had unknowingly been part of this cult for generations, celebrating not the birth of a savior, but the return of an ancient god—an entity that had long been forgotten in the shadows, waiting for the right moment to rise again.

Odin raised his hand, and the room seemed to pulse with dark energy. "You will join me, Emily, as the last sacrifice of your bloodline. You will serve me in the underworld, where you will never see the light again."

Her uncle, Richard, stood behind her, his face a mask of resolve. "It is our fate. It is the way of our people. You cannot escape what is inevitable."

With a sudden, violent motion, Odin's hand shot forward, and Emily felt herself pulled into the air, weightless, her body twisting as if caught in a vortex of darkness. The room vanished, and she was thrown into the cold embrace of the underworld, a place of eternal shadows.

And in that moment, as her screams were swallowed by the abyss, she understood: Christmas had never been about joy. It had always been about sacrifice. It had always been about Odin's return. And now, as the last of her line, she had fulfilled her role in the ancient pact, becoming a part of the eternal darkness.

The old gods had risen, and mankind's doom had arrived.

The Elves of Despair

The town of Ravensmoor had always been a quiet place, a town with a long history of strange occurrences and whispered secrets. It wasn't the kind of place where people openly discussed their fears, but if you knew where to look, you could hear the rumors—whispers about the cursed forest at the edge of town, about the strange noises that could be heard coming from the hills after dark, and about the old man who lived in the mansion on the hill, the one with the wild, untamed beard and an obsession with Christmas.

Nobody knew exactly where he had come from. Some said he was a former reclusive inventor; others said he was an ancient sorcerer, one who had long ago made a pact with dark forces. His name was seldom spoken, but everyone knew him as Old Kringle, the man who seemed to be the very embodiment of Christmas, yet left behind a sense of dread wherever he went.

Marcus had heard the stories all his life, but he had never truly believed them. He had grown up in Ravensmoor, and for most of his adulthood, he had worked as a carpenter, living a quiet, uneventful life. But that all changed the winter he received the letter.

It was postmarked from Ravensmoor, with no return address. Inside, there was only a single sentence: *Come to Kringle's workshop this Christmas Eve. We have much to show you.*

Curiosity gnawed at Marcus, and despite the unease that settled in his gut, he found himself walking up the long, snow-covered path toward the mansion at the edge of town. The trees that lined the way seemed darker than usual, their gnarled branches twisting into shapes that seemed almost human. The air was thick with the scent of pine and something else—something metallic, like the scent of blood.

When he finally reached the mansion, he was greeted by a single candle flickering in the window. He knocked on the door, and it creaked open almost immediately, revealing a tall, thin figure in a long coat and a snow-covered hat. His face was obscured by the shadows, but his voice was unmistakably deep and cold.

"Ah, Marcus. I've been expecting you."

The man, Old Kringle, ushered Marcus inside without another word. The moment he crossed the threshold, Marcus felt the temperature drop by several degrees. The air was thick with the smell of something foul, like rotting wood and stale sweat. Kringle led him through dark, winding hallways, past rooms that seemed to whisper of forgotten things. And then they came to a door at the end of a corridor, a large wooden door that was sealed tight with chains.

"This is where the magic happens," Kringle said with a smile that didn't reach his eyes. He motioned for Marcus to enter.

Marcus hesitated but stepped inside, his eyes widening at what he saw. The room was vast, filled with machinery and strange contraptions, some of them whirring softly, others standing still as if waiting for something. At the center of the room was a large, wooden workbench, covered in tools and scraps of metal, but it was the creatures working around the room that caught Marcus's attention.

At first, he thought they were elves—small, sprightly figures wearing ragged clothing, their eyes bright with an unnatural gleam as they scurried about the room, piecing together toys and gifts with unsettling precision. But as he watched them more closely, something didn't add up. Their movements were too quick, too jerky, like marionettes controlled by unseen strings. Their faces were twisted, their smiles too wide, their eyes far too dark.

Suddenly, one of them turned to face Marcus, and he froze. It was no elf—at least, not in any sense he had ever known. The creature's face was grotesque, its skin stretched tight over sharp, pointed bones. Its lips curled into a smile that was all teeth, and its eyes—black, empty voids—stared straight into his soul.

Before he could speak, Kringle's voice cut through the silence. "They're not what they seem, are they, Marcus?" He stepped closer, his breath cold in the air. "These are no simple helpers. These are the children of the abyss, demons bound to serve me, to build the toys and gifts that feed the ritual. You see, Christmas isn't just about giving. It's about taking, too."

Marcus's heart pounded in his chest as he tried to back away, but the door slammed shut behind him, trapping him in the room with the twisted creatures. The air felt thick, as though the very walls were closing in on him.

Kringle smiled again, that same cold, unfeeling smile. "I've waited for so long to share this with you. You think of Christmas as a time of joy, of innocence. But it is a time of blood and sacrifice. Every year, as people decorate their trees, as they give and receive their presents, they feed the dark forces that dwell in the hearts of the earth. I have been chosen to bring them into the light, to allow them to walk among us. And you, Marcus, are the final piece of the puzzle."

A chill ran down Marcus's spine as he turned to look at the creatures again. They were no longer working. They had stopped what they were doing and were slowly making their way toward him, their eyes fixed on him like hungry predators.

"What are you going to do to me?" Marcus whispered, his voice trembling.

Kringle chuckled, the sound hollow and distant. "You'll join them, of course. You'll help them complete their work. Just as you've always helped, in one way or another. We're all part of the same system, Marcus. We give, we take. And in the end, we all serve."

The creatures surrounded Marcus, their cold hands reaching out to pull him toward the workbench. He fought, but it was useless. They were too strong, their grip like iron as they dragged him across the room, their cold laughter echoing in his ears.

As they began to tie him down, his mind raced, but it was too late. The toys, the gifts, the rituals—none of it had ever been for joy. It had all been part of a far darker plan, one that went back centuries, one that had fed on the innocence of children and the greed of mankind.

The last thing Marcus saw before everything went black was the twisted, unholy smile of Old Kringle. And as the cold hands of the demons tightened around him, he understood the truth too late: Christmas was never about joy. It was about the harvest.

And no one ever left the workshop alive.

Krampus' Return

The cold wind howled through the streets of Heidelberg, whipping through the alleys and rattling the windows of the houses. Christmas had always been a time of joy in the small German town—families gathered, children eagerly awaited their gifts, and the scent of cinnamon and pine filled the air. But this year, something was different. Something darker. There was a feeling in the air, a subtle shift that no one could quite put their finger on, but all of them could sense.

For Anna, the change was most apparent in the look on her young son Lukas's face as he clutched his Christmas wish list. He had always been a lively child, his imagination as wild and free as his energy. But now, as the days drew closer to Christmas, Lukas had become quiet, withdrawn. He spoke less and less, his eyes constantly darting toward the shadows, as if watching something just out of view.

One night, as Anna tucked him into bed, she noticed something she hadn't before. Lukas's eyes weren't filled with the usual excitement about Christmas. They were wide with fear.

"Mama," he whispered, his voice trembling. "Do you think Krampus will come this year?"

Anna froze, a chill running down her spine at the mention of the creature. Krampus was a name passed down in the stories her grandmother used to tell her—an old legend, a tale of a terrifying demon who came to punish the wicked during the Christmas season. A creature with horns, a long, lolling tongue, and chains clinking as he dragged his sack full of misbehaving children to the underworld.

She had always thought of Krampus as a myth, something to scare children into being good during the holidays. But the more she thought about Lukas's question, the more uneasy she became. There was something about his tone, something in the way he asked that felt more than a child's passing curiosity.

"I think you're just imagining things, Lukas," Anna said, brushing the hair from his forehead and trying to offer him a comforting smile. "Krampus isn't real. He's just a story."

But deep down, Anna wasn't sure anymore. The old stories spoke of Krampus's return every Christmas, but this year, things felt... wrong. There were whispers in the town, murmurs from the older residents that Krampus wasn't a myth after all—that he was real, a herald of something far darker.

That night, Anna couldn't sleep. The wind outside howled like something alive, and every creak of the floorboards seemed magnified, echoing in her ears. Every time she closed her eyes, she saw flashes of dark, twisted shadows—horns and eyes glowing red, a figure moving in the night. The fear in Lukas's eyes replayed over and over again in her mind.

It was well past midnight when Anna heard it. A noise outside. A deep, guttural growl, like something waking from a long slumber. She rushed to the window, her heart racing, and peered out into the snow-covered street. The moon was high, casting long shadows across the ground, but there was no one there—nothing that should have been making the noise.

She dismissed it as the wind, trying to calm herself, but then she heard it again—a scraping sound, followed by a low, menacing chuckle. The sound seemed to be coming closer. Panic surged within her, and she turned away from the window, her breath coming in quick, shallow gasps.

"Mama?" Lukas's voice was small, fragile, from the other room. Anna's heart stopped. She had to protect him. Whatever was out there, it was after them, after their family. She ran to his room, but when she opened the door, her worst nightmare was realized. Lukas was sitting up in bed, staring at something invisible in the corner of the room. His face was pale, his eyes wide with terror.

"Mama, he's here..." Lukas whispered, his voice barely audible.

Anna turned slowly, fear constricting her chest as she followed his gaze to the corner of the room. There, standing in the shadows, was a figure—tall, twisted, with long horns curling from a dark, grotesque face. Its eyes glowed with an otherworldly red, and its tongue lolled out of its mouth like a serpent. It had chains wrapped around its body, dragging across the floor with a deafening clink as it took one slow, menacing step toward them.

The creature—Krampus—was real.

Anna's breath caught in her throat as the beast reached out, long claws scraping across the floorboards. Her mind raced, trying to make sense of what was happening. She had heard the stories, of course, but they were just stories, tales to frighten children. How could this be real? How could something so terrifying, so ancient, truly exist?

But Krampus's presence was undeniable. He was here, and he was not just a creature of myth. He was something far worse, something that had come for them, for their souls.

With a sudden, jarring movement, Krampus lunged forward, and in that moment, Anna knew there was no escape. The world seemed to slow as Krampus's hand clamped down on Lukas, lifting him from the bed with a strength far beyond anything human. Lukas screamed, but his voice was muffled by the horrible laughter that echoed through the room, the laughter of the demon who had returned to collect what was his.

Anna rushed forward, her mind screaming for a way to save her son, but it was too late. The room seemed to darken as Krampus's form loomed over them both, his chains rattling like a death knell.

"This is the price of your greed," Krampus growled, his voice like a thousand whispers. "You thought Christmas was a time for gifts, for joy. But it is a time for judgment, for reckoning. For every soul that has turned away from the truth, for every child left to rot in the sin of their parents' indulgence... I come for you."

And with that, the world went black.

When the authorities arrived the next morning, the house was eerily quiet. There were no signs of a struggle, no blood, no trace of the horror that had unfolded the night before. The only thing left behind was Lukas's wish list, crumpled and torn, with one last, chilling message scrawled at the bottom in red ink: *Krampus will return.*

The residents of Heidelberg were left to wonder if Krampus had truly come, or if it had been a nightmare. They whispered among themselves, certain that something dark had arrived that night. But they could never know the truth.

And every year, when Christmas drew near, the fear would return, as deep and quiet as the snow—because they knew that Krampus had not left. He was waiting, biding his time, ready to return again for those who had forgotten the true meaning of the season.

It wasn't about gifts, or joy, or indulgence. It was about judgment.

And none would escape it.

33

Satan's Sleigh

The town of Belgrave had always been the picture of peace. Nestled in the rolling hills of the countryside, it seemed untouched by the world's darker forces. It was the kind of place where Christmas felt eternal—where the scent of pine and the glow of holiday lights were constants. Every year, families gathered to celebrate, children eagerly anticipating the arrival of Santa Claus, believing him to be the jolly old man in a red suit who brought joy and gifts.

But this year, something was different. Something felt... wrong.

It began as a whisper—a strange rumor that spread quickly among the children. The older ones spoke in hushed tones, their eyes filled with something between fear and curiosity. They spoke of the sleigh, the one that flew through the night sky, delivering presents to the world's children. Only it wasn't Santa who rode in it this year. It was something else—something darker.

James, a young boy with a thirst for adventure, was among those who first heard the rumor. His friends had been talking about it at school, exchanging nervous glances as they dared each other to go outside and look for the sleigh. But James, with his usual curiosity and his disdain for what he saw as childish superstition, wasn't afraid. He decided to join them.

That Christmas Eve, just as the moon hung low in the sky and the stars twinkled coldly above, James and his friends gathered in the center of town. The streets were empty, save for the occasional flickering of a light in a window, the warmth of family gatherings behind closed doors. But they were here, in the shadows, waiting.

"It'll come," whispered Max, one of James's oldest friends. "I heard the sleigh is different this year. They say it's not Santa who's driving it."

James scoffed. "It's just a story. You're all just scared."

But as the minutes passed, and the night grew colder, James couldn't shake the sense that something was watching them. He looked up at the sky, half expecting to see a streak of red light cutting through the dark, the sound of sleigh bells ringing in the distance. But instead, there was nothing but silence.

Then, just as he was about to turn back, there was a sound—a distant, eerie jingling of bells. His heart skipped a beat. He turned to see the others, their faces pale and wide-eyed, all staring in the same direction. There, on the horizon, a dark shape appeared, growing larger and larger, and as it drew closer, James's blood turned to ice. It wasn't the cheerful sleigh he had grown up imagining, pulled by reindeer. This sleigh was different—black as night, with sharp, jagged edges that gleamed under the pale light of the moon. The reindeer, too, were not the innocent creatures of legend. They were twisted, their eyes glowing red, their antlers bent and malformed like wicked, gnarled branches.

The bells grew louder as the sleigh descended, its presence so overwhelming that the ground beneath James's feet seemed to shake. The sleigh landed silently, just in front of them, and the door opened.

"Who wants to see the world?" came a voice, low and guttural, like thunder, but there was no one in sight. The voice seemed to come from the very air around them, filling their minds, their souls, compelling them to step forward.

James felt his body moving without his control, his feet pulling him toward the sleigh. He glanced at Max, who stood frozen, his face pale with fear, but his eyes—his eyes were glazed over, like he was already lost. The others had already stepped forward, one by one, as if some invisible force had taken hold of them. They were no longer the children James had known. They were husks, puppets of some ancient power that controlled their every movement.

"Don't!" James wanted to shout, but his voice was lost in the wind. Instead, he stepped forward, unable to stop himself. His heart raced as he reached the edge of the sleigh, his fingers trembling as they brushed against the cold wood.

And then, the door to the sleigh opened wide, revealing an interior cloaked in darkness. He could hear whispers from within—voices speaking in tongues he could not understand. The air grew thick, and a foul odor wafted from the sleigh, the stench of decay, of something far beyond death.

"Come with us, James," the voice intoned, but this time, it was different—it was no longer a voice in the air, but a voice in his head, pulling him, urging him forward. "Come, and see what the world truly is."

He could feel himself shaking, his mind fighting against the pull, but there was no escape. His feet moved, dragging him inside the sleigh, and as he stepped into the dark interior, he felt the chill of the void surround him. The door slammed shut behind him, and the sleigh lifted off the ground, shooting upward into the sky at a speed so fast, James felt as though his very soul was being ripped from his body.

The world below disappeared in an instant, replaced by swirling mists, endless and dark. The sleigh hurtled through a space that was not the world he knew, a place where time and reality twisted together like a nightmare. He could hear the laughter of children, but it was not joyous. It was hollow, tinged with terror. He turned to see the others, his friends, but they were no longer children. Their faces were gaunt, their eyes hollow, like something had drained the life from them.

"Where are we going?" James whispered, his voice shaking.

"To a place where your sins will be paid for," came the response. The voice was deep, ancient—almost familiar. "This is no mere sleigh, James. This is a vessel, a ship that carries souls to their rightful place. You were foolish to chase after me, foolish to follow."

The sleigh jerked violently, and James's stomach churned. He felt his mind slipping, his thoughts growing fuzzy as the air around him turned to ice. The others—his friends—were no longer moving. They were suspended, their bodies stiff, their eyes staring blankly ahead. It was then that James realized with growing horror: they were not alive. They were never alive again.

The sleigh suddenly stopped, and James was thrust forward, landing hard on the ground. When he opened his eyes, he saw that they were no longer in the sky. They were in a vast, barren wasteland, a land of fire and ash. In the distance, he saw a figure, dark and looming, standing before a massive throne. Its eyes glowed red, burning with an intensity that made James's skin crawl. It was then that he understood.

The voice, the pull—the sleigh—it had all been a ruse, a trap to bring him here, to this place ruled by the one who waited for them all: Satan himself.

"There is no Christmas here," the voice spoke again. "There is only eternity. And you will join the others in servitude, forever."

And as the darkness closed in, swallowing him whole, James understood the lesson too late: Christmas was never about gifts, or joy, or the spirit of giving. It was about power. And those who believed in the myth of Santa Claus, who followed the lies, were doomed to pay the price in the end.

The sleigh was no gift-giver. It was a trap. And in the end, no one ever returned.

The Darkest Night

It was the kind of Christmas Eve that seemed perfect in its stillness. The wind outside howled through the trees, but inside, the Thompson family sat gathered by the fire. The house, bathed in the warm glow of Christmas lights and the scent of roasting chestnuts, seemed like the embodiment of everything Christmas was supposed to be—peaceful, joyful, full of warmth and love. Yet, despite the festive decorations and the laughter that filled the air, something felt wrong.

It had started earlier in the evening, when the clock struck midnight. At first, there was no reason for the unease that crept into Clara Thompson's chest. It was just the long shadows of the night, she reasoned. But as the minutes passed, the darkness outside seemed to thicken, pressing closer to the windows, obscuring the world beyond.

Clara stood and walked to the window, pressing her hand against the cold glass. Snow was falling in thick, heavy flakes, blanketing the world in white. It should have been a comforting sight, but something about the way the snow fell—endlessly, without pause—struck her as wrong. The world outside had become eerily silent, as if the snow itself was muting every sound.

"Mom?" Her son Ben's voice broke through her thoughts. "Can we open our presents now?"

She turned back to find her children—Ben, Emma, and little Jack—gathered around the Christmas tree, their faces bright with excitement. The warmth of their smiles should have soothed her, but instead, she felt a strange sense of dread wash over her.

"Sure," Clara said, forcing a smile as she joined them by the tree. The presents were wrapped neatly, sparkling with ribbons and bows, their shiny surfaces catching the light from the fire. She didn't want to be the one to dampen the holiday cheer, so she sat down beside them and began handing out the gifts. But as the moments passed, Clara's unease only grew. The air in the room was still, too still, and as the children tore through their presents, her eyes kept drifting back to the window.

The clock on the wall ticked loudly, but it felt... off. Time seemed to be stretching, like the hands of the clock were dragging through thick mud. Clara glanced at the time. It was 12:15. She blinked. Hadn't it been 12:15 for the past twenty minutes?

"Mom, look!" Ben held up a toy car, his eyes shining. "It's just like the one I wanted!"

"That's great, honey," Clara said, trying to focus on him. But the odd sensation didn't let up. The seconds were dragging, the night stretching on in unnatural ways.

She stood up, suddenly needing to move, needing to break the stillness. "I'll check on dinner," she murmured, excusing herself from the room. As she walked into the kitchen, her heart was hammering in her chest. She opened the oven, only to find it was empty. The smell of roasting chestnuts, which had filled the house just an hour before, was gone. The kitchen was cold, colder than it should have been, despite the fire in the living room.

Clara walked to the window above the sink and looked outside. The snow was still falling, but now it seemed to swirl in unnatural patterns, twisting in the wind. She stared at it, feeling her breath quicken.

Something wasn't right.

She turned around quickly, rushing back to the living room, but the moment she entered, she froze. The children were still sitting in front of the tree, but their faces had changed. They weren't smiling anymore. They were staring at the presents, unmoving, their eyes wide, unblinking, and filled with terror.

"Mom," Emma whispered, her voice trembling, "why is the sun still down?"

Clara turned, her eyes wide with panic. It was true. Outside the windows, the sky was still dark, and the snow continued to fall, as though time had stopped.

The clock on the wall read 12:30.

Clara's heart dropped into her stomach. The same time, the same minute. How had the time not passed? Hadn't she just seen it move forward? She glanced at the door. The house was too still, the air too thick. It was like they were trapped in this moment, forever suspended in time.

"Mom," Ben said again, his voice unnervingly calm. "I heard something. Up on the roof."

Clara's blood ran cold. The roof? She turned and walked to the door, opening it cautiously. The cold air hit her like a slap to the face, but when she stepped outside, her breath froze in the air. There was no sound, no crunch of snow beneath her feet. The world was blanketed in white, the landscape muted, as though it had been sucked into a void.

Then she heard it.

A low rumbling, like the sound of something large and heavy moving overhead. It started slowly, and then it grew louder, more distinct.

The unmistakable sound of sleigh bells.

Clara's pulse quickened as she looked up. The sleigh appeared above her—an impossibly large, dark silhouette in the sky, the sound of the bells growing louder with each passing second. She could see nothing pulling the sleigh, but the shape of it was unmistakable. It was a shadow, but it wasn't a shadow from the night—it was a blackness of its own, suffocating, like the absence of light itself. The bells rang louder, shaking the very air around her. She stumbled back, her heart pounding, her breath shallow.

The sleigh continued its descent, a dark figure inside watching her. Santa's face, or what had once been Santa's face, loomed in the darkness, his eyes glowing with a cold, malevolent fire. And as the sleigh touched down on the ground, Clara saw the figure's mouth move, forming words she couldn't hear, only feel in her bones.

"Welcome to the longest night," the air seemed to whisper. "You will never see the light again."

The darkness around her deepened, and the world seemed to pull in on itself. The clock in the house chimed loudly, but the sound was distorted, like it was coming from deep under water. Clara ran back inside, but when she entered the living room, her heart froze.

The children were gone. The tree was gone. Everything was gone. The fire in the hearth had long since burned out, and the house was empty, cold, and devoid of life.

It was then that Clara realized with a sickening clarity: they were trapped in the night, forever. Time had stopped, the world had stopped, and they were bound in the unending darkness, just as Santa's twisted influence had always meant.

The last thing she felt before the darkness swallowed her whole was the weight of time itself, pressing down on her, suffocating her, pulling her into the eternal night. There was no escape. There was only the endless, ever-present darkness.

And Christmas had become their damnation.

A Coal Black Christmas

Every year, the box arrived. An unmarked package, plain and nondescript, left quietly on the doorstep of one unsuspecting person. Its presence went unnoticed by the world, but for the recipient, it was the beginning of a nightmare they could never escape. This year, the box found its way to Derek, a man whose life was a routine of mediocrity, lost ambitions, and buried regrets.

Derek had never been one for superstition. He didn't believe in signs or omens, much less things like the old stories about a coal-black Christmas. But when the box appeared on his doorstep that cold December morning, something stirred deep inside him—a sickly feeling he couldn't shake. It was Christmas Eve, and he had just returned from the empty apartment where his family once lived. There had been no reason to decorate or celebrate. His wife had left him two months ago, and his son had stayed with her.

He wasn't sure what had driven him to open the box that day. Maybe it was the emptiness inside him, or perhaps it was curiosity. Inside the box, wrapped in thick, crinkled black paper, was a small coal. It was smooth, dark, and unnaturally heavy for its size. Derek held it in his palm, feeling an odd warmth radiating from it. A strange compulsion gripped him, but he couldn't understand why.

He placed it on the kitchen table and made a cup of coffee. The warmth from the coal lingered in the air like a whisper. Something was wrong, but Derek couldn't pinpoint it. His mind began to race with thoughts of his failures, his past, his broken relationships. He couldn't shake the feeling that this coal was tied to something deeper—something darker.

That night, as he lay in bed staring at the ceiling, the world outside seemed to darken in tandem with his thoughts. He woke to the sound of a distant knock on his door, followed by a soft voice—almost like a hiss. When he opened his eyes, the room was empty. He checked the door, but no one was there. It was as though the night had become oppressive, suffocating in its silence.

The next morning, the box was back, sitting in the same spot. It was almost as if it had never left. Another coal, darker, more twisted than the last, lay inside. Derek felt a surge of panic, but the curiosity gnawed at him, forcing his hands to reach for the coal again. As soon as his fingers touched it, the temperature dropped. He could feel the shadows of something watching him, pressing in from all sides, even though the house was still and empty. The air thickened, and a deep voice reverberated in his chest.

"You have been chosen."

The room spun, the lights flickering as the voice echoed. Derek staggered back, clutching his chest. His head buzzed with an overwhelming sense of dread, the weight of the box now sinking into his bones. He couldn't understand what was happening. The walls closed in, and his vision blurred as the voice inside his mind grew louder, more insistent.

"You have failed. Now, you must pay."

With a wrenching motion, Derek found himself thrown to the ground. His limbs locked, frozen, as though invisible chains bound him. He was no longer in his apartment. The walls had dissolved into a vast, empty void—a place that seemed to stretch on forever, a land where time had no meaning. The ground beneath him was cold, like a tomb. Above him, a figure loomed in the darkness—tall, shadowy, and formless, but exuding a suffocating presence.

"You have been chosen," the voice repeated, this time closer, the words sent deep into his soul.

"Who are you?" Derek gasped, his breath shallow, chest tight. His mind raced with questions, with disbelief, but the figure remained silent, only drawing closer.

A cold laugh echoed through the void.

"You know who I am," the voice purred. "The lies you've told yourself. The people you've betrayed. The ones you left behind."

Derek's throat tightened as memories rushed through his mind. The lies to his wife, the neglect of his son, the times he failed to be the man he promised he would be. They were all here, in the dark, twisted and warped. This was the price of his selfishness, the weight of his failures.

"You've been hiding from the truth for too long. Now, it's time to face the consequences." The figure extended its hand toward Derek, and he felt his body grow cold, as if the very life was draining from him. "You wanted freedom from responsibility. Now you'll understand that there's a price to be paid for the choices you make."

Derek wanted to scream, to resist, but the words caught in his throat. His body felt numb as he struggled against the pull of the darkness, the weight of his own guilt and remorse pressing him further into the abyss.

But there was no escape. The ground beneath him cracked open, and he fell through, deeper and deeper into the blackness. The shadows clung to him, suffocating him with the weight of his decisions, the years of avoiding responsibility, of chasing after hollow pleasures. He had spent his life pretending the darkness didn't exist, but it had been waiting for him, waiting to collect what was owed.

The last thing Derek heard, before everything went silent, was the soft, mocking sound of a coal cracking. And then, nothing.

Derek's body was never found. No one ever discovered where the box had come from or where it had gone. His disappearance became just another whispered mystery in the town. But those who knew him couldn't shake the feeling that something far darker than a missing person was behind it all.

The box had been a gift, after all—a gift that came with a price. The cold, black coal had been the first clue. And as the years passed, as Christmas came and went, the lesson remained: there is always a price for the things we try to bury, for the choices we make in the shadows. And sometimes, when the darkness comes calling, there is no escape.

Satan's Naughty List

The Smith family had always taken Christmas seriously. It was their one time of year to gather, to celebrate, and to forget the trivialities of the rest of the year. Henry, the father, was always the one to decorate the house with meticulous care, spending hours wrapping the tree with lights and ornaments. His wife, Evelyn, prepared the food, making sure everything was perfect for their two children, Olivia and Ryan. Despite their imperfections and occasional arguments, there was a sense of love that bound them during this season.

But this Christmas was different.

It started with an unusual package that arrived one week before Christmas. It was a thick, old-fashioned envelope, sealed with red wax, and it bore no return address. Henry had been the one to open it, only to find a yellowed piece of parchment inside, inscribed in an elegant yet unsettling hand:

"For the Smith family, the time has come to pay for your sins."

Henry stared at the words, unsure of their meaning. There was no signature, no sender, only those cryptic words. He dismissed it as a prank, perhaps something from one of the neighborhood kids trying to spook them. But Evelyn had a different feeling. She was unnerved, and for good reason. She had grown up hearing whispers about Christmas legends that went far beyond the jolly figure of Santa Claus. Her grandmother had told her dark stories of how Santa's list wasn't just a record of good and bad children. It was a ledger for something far more sinister—a ledger where Satan himself kept track of those who had strayed too far from grace.

That night, after the children had gone to bed, Evelyn couldn't shake the feeling that something was terribly wrong. The image of the parchment kept replaying in her mind, and a chill crept up her spine when she thought of her own past—the lies, the mistakes, the regrets. She had never truly forgiven herself for the things she'd done, and she feared that whatever this package was, it wasn't just a harmless joke.

She couldn't sleep. She lay in bed, staring at the ceiling, her mind racing, when she heard Henry's footsteps downstairs. Curious, she followed him, and as she descended the staircase, she found him at the kitchen table, staring at something with a look of dread on his face.

"What is it?" Evelyn asked, her voice trembling.

Henry didn't look up. His hand was shaking as he pointed to the table, to a large, leather-bound book lying open.

Evelyn's heart stopped as she saw the name at the top of the page. It was their name. *The Smith family.*

"What is this?" she whispered, a sense of cold terror creeping into her chest.

"It's a list," Henry muttered, his voice distant. "A list of names, written in this book. Some are marked 'naughty,' others 'nice,' but..."

His words trailed off as his eyes fell on the next line—*"The Smith Family: Naughty."*

There was no explanation, no reason why. Just that one damning word: *Naughty.*

"Henry... what does this mean?" Evelyn whispered, though she already knew the answer deep in her gut.

"I don't know. But this—this doesn't feel like some prank. This is something else. Something..." He trailed off, his eyes widening as he flipped through the pages, revealing countless other names, written in an elegant, precise hand. But each page seemed to have more than just the names—next to many of them were symbols that Evelyn couldn't understand.

"What do we do?" she asked, her voice barely audible.

"We need to find out what this is. Where it came from," Henry said, closing the book. "We can't ignore it."

The two of them stood there in silence for a moment, the weight of the book between them. Outside, the snow began to fall, as though the world outside had become a blur, empty and cold. The silence in the room seemed to stretch on forever.

As they sat back down at the table, trying to make sense of the mystery before them, there was a loud knock at the door. Evelyn froze. Henry's eyes shot to her, filled with dread.

"Who could that be?" she asked, her voice tight.

"I don't know," Henry replied, his gaze shifting to the door. He got up slowly and walked toward it, cautiously peering through the peephole.

His face went pale as he opened the door.

There, standing on the threshold, was a man in a long black coat, his face obscured by a wide-brimmed hat. He was tall, with a dark presence that seemed to consume the space around him.

"Can I help you?" Henry asked, his voice trembling.

"I've come for what's mine," the man said in a deep, gravelly voice. His words seemed to vibrate with an eerie resonance.

Henry's blood ran cold. The man stepped forward, pushing the door open slightly, his eyes locking with Henry's.

"You've been on the list for years. Now, the time has come. The payment is due."

Before Henry could respond, the man stepped aside and gestured toward the snow-filled night. At first, Henry didn't understand. But then he saw it—the sleigh. It wasn't like any sleigh he had seen before. It was black, unnaturally large, and the reindeer were twisted, with glowing red eyes. The man stepped aside, revealing the creature behind him.

And there, inside the sleigh, sat Santa—or rather, what had once been Santa. His eyes were hollow, filled with an ancient malevolence, and his smile was twisted, more sinister than any jolly figure should have been.

"The bargain has been made," the man said, his hand outstretched. "It's time for you to join the others."

Henry staggered back, his legs trembling. His mind reeled, the book's warning now a terrifying reality. This wasn't some fantasy. It wasn't a joke. The ledger was real, and they had been on the wrong list for decades.

"No... no..." Henry whispered, but the man's hand grabbed his arm with a strength that no human should have possessed.

"There is no escape," the man said, his voice a low growl. "The price for your sins has been paid, and now you will join those who are long lost. It is your turn to pay the price."

As Henry and Evelyn were dragged out into the snow, they realized too late that Christmas, the holiday they had so cherished, had never been about joy. It was about control, about choosing who would be taken, who would be left behind. And they had been on the wrong side of the ledger all along.

The sleigh took off into the cold night, and the last thing they saw was the twisted face of Santa, his eyes filled with hollow judgment, as the darkness swallowed them whole.

And in the end, the lesson was clear: the price of ignoring your own darkness is steep, and sometimes, there's no way to escape the consequences of your choices.

The Grin of Evil

Dr. Adrian Fisher was no stranger to the human mind. As a psychiatrist, he had spent years dissecting the twisted layers of human behavior, searching for patterns in the chaos that made people tick. He had treated everyone from the severely depressed to the violently psychotic, and his expertise was widely respected in his field. But it was Christmas that intrigued him the most—the psychological phenomenon of Santa Claus.

To most, Santa was a simple figure of joy, a benevolent old man with a round belly and a jolly laugh. But to Fisher, there was something unsettling about the figure. Every year, as December approached, his mind would wander to the same question: Why did Santa's smile seem so perfect, so inviting, yet so strangely hollow? There was something in the way his eyes shone—too bright, too wide—like a mask too tightly pulled across an ancient, evil face.

Fisher had never been able to dismiss it. His own Christmas memories, those happy moments of childhood, were tainted by a sense of unease whenever he thought about Santa. His own father had been a stoic, distant figure, and Santa had always seemed like an enigma—too perfect, too reliable. And yet, there was something wrong about him, something that Fisher couldn't quite explain.

This year, as Christmas approached once again, Fisher decided to finally confront it. He had the perfect excuse—he was writing a book on the psychology of holiday figures, using Santa as a case study. It was a brilliant idea, he thought. After all, Santa had become a cultural icon, universally loved and trusted. But Fisher wasn't interested in the myth itself. He wanted to peel back the layers and expose the truth beneath. There was something hidden there, something he knew would be disturbing.

He spent weeks poring over old texts, analyzing historical references to the man in red. He read about the origins of Saint Nicholas, the transformation into the modern-day Santa, and the evolution of his image. But it was the old illustrations—the ones from centuries ago—that truly caught his attention. The depictions of Santa had once been darker, more mysterious, even frightening. In some of the oldest images, Santa was a tall, looming figure, with eyes that seemed too sharp, too calculating. The modern version, Fisher realized, was a sanitized, watered-down version of something far more sinister.

One evening, as Fisher was researching late into the night, he came across a peculiar piece of footage. It was an old black-and-white clip, poorly lit, from a Christmas party filmed in the early 1900s. It showed a man dressed as Santa, his face obscured by the thick fur of his costume, but his eyes were visible—bright, gleaming, unnaturally wide. As the jolly man laughed and handed out presents to the children, Fisher couldn't help but notice the faint twitch at the corner of his mouth, the way his smile seemed almost too exaggerated, too much.

The camera zoomed in on his face as he turned to the camera, and Fisher felt a cold shiver run down his spine. The man's smile widened, not in a warm, joyful way, but in something darker, like a grimace. His eyes—those eyes—stared straight into the lens, not in the way a man would look into a camera, but in a way that felt far too intimate, far too knowing.

Fisher froze the frame, staring at the image. The longer he looked, the more it seemed to distort. The man's features blurred, and the grin... it stretched wider, more grotesque. Fisher blinked and rubbed his eyes, but the grin remained, an unnatural mockery of happiness. It was as though the man in the footage knew something the rest of the world didn't, something deeply unsettling.

The smile, the eyes—it was as though Santa was a mask, and something far more sinister was beneath the surface, something ancient and powerful, waiting to be released. Fisher's mind raced, his thoughts spinning. What was this? Was it just the product of his overactive imagination, or was something truly horrific hidden beneath the myth?

The more he thought about it, the more convinced he became that Santa's smile wasn't just a symbol of good will. It was a mask, a façade, a lie. It was a perfect illusion to hide something far darker. He had seen it in the footage, and he could see it now, in every image of Santa he had ever seen. There was something fundamentally wrong about the jolly man, something that didn't belong in the world of children's dreams.

As Christmas Eve drew near, Fisher's obsession with the smile grew. He started to see it everywhere—on billboards, in stores, in the faces of people he passed on the street. The grin of evil was everywhere, hidden in plain sight. Fisher could feel it creeping into his own psyche, slowly unraveling his mind. He couldn't sleep, couldn't eat, and every time he closed his eyes, he saw the smile—twisted, mocking, inescapable.

Then, on Christmas Eve, it happened. Fisher sat alone in his office, surrounded by papers, empty coffee cups, and the harsh glow of his desk lamp. The clock ticked closer to midnight, and he felt the weight of his own thoughts closing in on him. He couldn't shake the image of that grin, that unsettling, perfect smile that seemed to stretch forever.

As the clock struck twelve, the door to his office creaked open. Fisher looked up, his heart racing. He expected to see his assistant, but instead, standing in the doorway, was a figure.

The man wore a red suit, a thick fur trim hanging around his shoulders, and a white beard that obscured most of his face. But the eyes—those eyes—shone with an intensity that made Fisher's blood run cold. The smile, that wide, perfect grin, spread across his face like a grotesque parody of warmth.

"Dr. Fisher," the figure said in a voice that was both deep and hollow, "you've discovered the truth, haven't you?"

Fisher's mind screamed at him to run, but he was paralyzed, unable to move, unable to speak. The figure stepped forward, its eyes never leaving him, the grin widening. Fisher tried to fight back, but the figure's presence was overwhelming, suffocating.

"Do you understand now, Dr. Fisher?" the figure whispered. "Santa is no gift-giver. He is a harbinger. A mask for something far darker. And now, you've seen it too clearly. You've uncovered the truth beneath the illusion."

The figure moved closer, and as it did, Fisher felt his mind slipping, unraveling like a thread in the wind. His heart raced as he saw the grin stretch further, impossibly wide, until it consumed the entire face, leaving nothing but darkness behind it.

And as the darkness closed in on him, Fisher understood the truth—Santa was not a symbol of joy. He was a harbinger of doom, a mask that concealed the evil that had always lurked beneath, waiting for the right moment to reveal itself.

And now, Fisher had seen it. There was no escape.

The last thing Fisher saw, as the grin swallowed him whole, was the perfect, terrifying smile that would haunt his every waking moment.

In the end, he realized: some masks were never meant to be removed.

The Disappearing Christmas Spirit

Every year, as the calendar turned to December, the town of Ashford grew quieter. The streets, once bustling with the cheer of holiday shoppers and children eagerly awaiting the arrival of Christmas, had become eerily still. It was as though the joy that had once filled the air had simply vanished, dissipating like smoke in the wind. The Christmas spirit, as people called it, seemed to grow fainter with each passing year.

Tom Harris, a man in his early forties with a quiet demeanor and a keen sense of observation, had noticed the change more than most. His entire life had been marked by the joy of the season, from the twinkling lights adorning houses to the laughter that filled homes on Christmas Eve. But in recent years, he had felt it slipping away. The excitement of children had diminished. People had grown more focused on consumerism, treating Christmas like any other commercial holiday, rather than a time for warmth, family, and magic.

He couldn't pinpoint the exact moment when things began to change, but it seemed that the more children "believed" in Santa Claus, the more something felt wrong in the world. Every year, the joy grew smaller, more fleeting. And the dark shadows that loomed at the edges of the season became harder to ignore. There was a heaviness that hung over Ashford, a quiet desperation that grew with each Christmas.

One particularly cold December evening, Tom sat alone in his small apartment, nursing a drink, his mind preoccupied with thoughts of the Christmas spirit's decline. He remembered a time when belief in Santa Claus brought a certain lightness to the world, a time when innocence seemed invincible. But now, the magic seemed gone, replaced by cold indifference and selfishness. The question that haunted him was simple—what had happened to that spirit? Where had it gone?

His curiosity, which had always been a driving force in his life, pushed him to investigate. The more he observed, the more he became convinced that there was more to the disappearance of the Christmas spirit than just time or apathy. Something sinister was at work, feeding off the very belief that kept Christmas alive.

Tom began by asking questions—quietly, almost imperceptibly, to those around him. He visited local stores, listened to parents, talked to the elderly, and observed children. He learned things he hadn't expected. There was a pervasive sense of unease in the town, one that grew sharper and more noticeable each year. Children were no longer filled with wonder at the thought of Santa Claus; instead, they were quickly taught to move on from him as they grew older, as though the idea of magic and wonder was something to outgrow.

But there was one thing that stood out in nearly every conversation he had. Children, when asked about Santa Claus, would still smile faintly, as if there was a trace of belief left within them. But when Tom looked closely, he saw something more. Something dark. Something malevolent lurking beneath their innocent eyes.

After weeks of research, he came across something that made his stomach churn. A forgotten manuscript, buried in the archives of Ashford's library, spoke of the true origin of Santa Claus—an origin far darker than anything Tom had imagined. It wasn't merely a jolly old man who brought gifts and joy. No, Santa, as it turned out, was a symbol of something much older, much more dangerous. The manuscript revealed that every time children believed in Santa, they unknowingly empowered a much older being—a demonic force who had long ago made a pact with humanity. The belief in Santa wasn't just a harmless tradition—it was a ritual that fed this force, giving it power to shape the world, to bend it to its will.

The more he read, the more Tom's blood ran cold. This was no innocent figure. Santa Claus, as he had come to be known, was merely a front, a way to bind humanity's soul to a darker fate. The Christmas spirit, the joy and warmth that had once filled homes, was simply a façade. Beneath it, in the shadows, the demonic force of Satan was waiting, growing stronger with every child's belief. The more they believed, the more power they gave it.

Tom tried to push the manuscript aside, but the truth was too undeniable. He had to find out more. He had to stop it. The thought of it gnawed at him as Christmas Eve approached. He knew what he had to do. He had to find a way to sever the connection, to stop the belief from growing any stronger.

On Christmas Eve, as the town of Ashford prepared for its annual celebration, Tom followed his research to the last step. The manuscript had described an old ritual, one that would sever the demonic bond that had been woven into the fabric of Christmas itself. It required a confrontation—an act of complete rejection. He had to stand in the heart of the town square, on the night of the longest night of the year, and declare to the heavens that he would no longer believe. He had to shatter the illusion once and for all.

As midnight approached, Tom stood in the square, the empty streets echoing with the silence of a town that had long since abandoned its joy. He raised his arms to the sky, shouting out the words of rejection he had read in the manuscript. "I do not believe! I refuse the magic, I refuse the illusion! There is no Santa! There is no magic, no spirit, only darkness!"

For a moment, the wind howled around him, and he thought for a second that something had changed. But then, something far worse happened. The ground beneath him began to tremble, the air thick with a stifling, oppressive weight. The darkness around him deepened, swirling into a vortex. And there, in the center of the square, the figure of Santa Claus appeared—not as the jolly old man, but as a towering, monstrous entity, its grin wide and twisted, its eyes black voids of emptiness.

"You fool," the voice of the figure boomed, its voice not jolly, but filled with an ancient malice. "You think you can stop it? You think you can undo the belief? The spirit is already gone. You have fed me. You have made me real. And now, you shall see what comes after."

Tom's heart pounded in his chest as he realized the truth. The belief was never the source of the Christmas spirit. It had been the source of the destruction all along. The magic, the joy, the warmth—it was all a trap. And now, in his desperation to stop it, he had only hastened its end.

The ground beneath him cracked open, and the darkness swallowed him whole, pulling him into an eternal void.

And in the end, the lesson was clear: the Christmas spirit was never about hope or joy. It was about the power of belief—and how easily it could be twisted into something far darker.

The Jolly Demon

Clara Mitchell had always loved Christmas. The season of giving, the scent of pine needles and cinnamon in the air, the joy of family gathered around a well-decorated tree—everything about it felt magical. It was a time when her family came together, when the stresses of life seemed to fade away, and the warmth of the season filled every corner of her home. But that was before. Before she found the toy.

It had arrived on Christmas Eve, tucked under the tree, with no tag, no name, no explanation. Clara hadn't even noticed it at first, distracted by the chaos of the holiday. Her husband, Daniel, had been running late for a business meeting, and the kids—Jacob and Lily—were full of energy, tearing through the house in a frenzy of excitement. The toy sat quietly in the corner, its bright red color standing out against the sea of other, more traditional gifts. It looked like a jolly little clown—well-worn, its fabric faded, with an unsettling smile sewn onto its face.

It wasn't until after the kids had gone to bed that Clara noticed the toy again. It was placed carefully on the armchair by the fireplace, as if someone had put it there deliberately. At first, Clara thought it was one of the kids' gifts they had forgotten to unwrap, but when she picked it up, a strange shiver ran down her spine. It felt cold, too cold for something left under the tree. Its smile seemed almost too wide, too forced.

She set it back down, trying to brush off the unease that crept into her chest. But sleep eluded her that night. As the clock struck midnight, she heard faint sounds—a giggle, low and menacing—coming from the living room. Heart racing, she crept out of bed and slowly made her way toward the source of the sound.

There, sitting in the dim light of the fireplace, was the toy. Its eyes seemed to glimmer in the dark, its smile stretching impossibly wide. And then it spoke, a voice so low and chilling that Clara's blood ran cold.

"Santa is watching."

The words sent a shock of terror through her, and she dropped the toy in a rush of panic. The sound of it hitting the ground echoed through the empty house, and the air around her felt heavy, oppressive. Clara's breath quickened, and her heart thudded painfully in her chest. This wasn't right. None of this felt right.

She tried to shake it off, but the unease grew with every passing moment. The next morning, she found herself telling Daniel about the toy, but he laughed it off. "You've been working too hard, Clara. It's just a toy, nothing more."

But it was more than that. Clara could feel it in her bones. She watched the kids play with the toy over the next few days, their laughter growing louder, more unsettling. Jacob, usually shy and reserved, had become strangely obsessed with it. He carried it everywhere, even to school. His behavior grew erratic, his eyes darting nervously, and Clara noticed the dark circles under his eyes. He wasn't sleeping.

It was Lily's turn next. One evening, Clara found her daughter staring at the toy, her small fingers twitching as if trying to hold back something terrible. Her lips moved silently, mouthing words Clara couldn't hear. When Clara called out to her, Lily jerked back, her face pale and terrified.

"I—I don't want it anymore, Mommy," Lily whispered, pointing at the toy with trembling hands. "It's bad, Mommy. It wants us to go with it."

Clara's heart sank. She could feel the weight of something ancient and evil pressing down on her family. She didn't know how or why, but the toy had a power over her children—something insidious, something she couldn't understand. The more they interacted with it, the more the dark energy it radiated seemed to twist their minds, pulling them closer to something unholy.

That night, she made a decision. She had to destroy it, get rid of it once and for all before it claimed any more of her family. She snuck into the living room, where the toy sat, grinning up at her from the corner. But as her hand reached for it, the room grew colder, and a voice, deep and resonant, filled her ears.

"You cannot stop it," the voice rumbled. "You are already mine."

Clara's hand recoiled, but she couldn't tear her eyes away from the toy. It wasn't just a simple artifact of some childhood memory. It was a gateway. The toy had been touched by something far darker than she had imagined. It had been crafted with the intent of pulling its owners into an ancient ritual, a ritual that promised the souls of those who believed in Santa to Satan himself.

She tried to scream, but the words were caught in her throat. It was as if the very air around her had become thick with evil, with despair. She looked toward the stairs, where Jacob and Lily were sleeping, but she knew it was already too late. The toy had been a vessel, a way for the dark force to latch onto their souls, and now it had them. It had taken them, just as it had taken her.

Before she could move, a cold wind swept through the room, and the lights flickered. The toy began to rock on its own, its grin widening impossibly. Then, just as quickly, everything went black.

When Clara awoke, she was standing in the same room, but it was empty. The house was eerily silent. She stumbled through the rooms, calling out for her children, but there was no response. The furniture had been rearranged, the air stale with the smell of something ancient. It was as though time itself had shifted, and in the void where her family had been, only emptiness remained.

Then she saw it—a shadow in the corner of her vision. She turned, and there, standing at the doorway, was the toy. It was smiling at her, its eyes dark and void of life.

"Santa has claimed you all," the voice echoed, coming from the toy. "And now, you serve him, forever."

Clara collapsed to her knees, understanding too late that there was no escape. The toy was not just a simple relic of childhood; it had been a bridge, a gateway. And now, her family was lost, claimed by the very darkness they had unwittingly invited into their home.

And as Clara's soul was dragged into the shadows, the lesson was clear: the things we believe in without question can be the very things that destroy us.

The Sinister Santa

It was the strange, unsettling quiet that first made Lydia notice it. Every Christmas, as the first snowflakes began to fall, the small town of Windlake grew eerily still. The air, usually filled with the chatter of holiday preparations and the hum of busy shoppers, seemed to lose its sound. Streets that would normally be alive with families rushing between stores were now empty. Houses sat dark, their lights dimmed, even though Christmas was just days away.

Lydia had always loved Christmas. It was a time of warmth and togetherness, a time to reconnect with family and friends. But in Windlake, something had changed over the years. No one spoke of it, not directly, but the discomfort was palpable. No matter how festive the decorations were, no matter how cheerful the songs that played in the stores, the town felt off.

She wasn't the only one who had noticed it. Her friends—Max, Eva, and Brian—had also been growing increasingly uneasy with each passing year. It wasn't just the silence; it was something deeper. Their town, once known for its lively Christmas spirit, had grown lifeless. People no longer smiled the same way. Children no longer rushed to the windows to see Santa's sleigh, and adults seemed to keep their distance from each other. The magic that Christmas was supposed to bring had all but disappeared.

This year, the four of them decided to investigate. Something was wrong, and they were determined to find out what it was. They had always been close, growing up together in Windlake, and they remembered the town's Christmases of old, when the streets buzzed with excitement, when every corner seemed alive with the energy of the season.

On Christmas Eve, the town was quieter than ever. Max, Eva, Brian, and Lydia met at the local diner, a small building at the edge of town, where they had spent countless hours as teenagers. They sat around a table, their mugs of coffee untouched, as they discussed their plans.

"We need to find out what's causing this," Brian said, his voice low, almost a whisper. "Every year it gets worse. We can't keep pretending that it's just a coincidence."

"I know what you mean," Lydia replied, glancing around the diner. The only other people there were a couple sitting quietly in the corner, barely speaking to one another. "It's as if the town's been... hypnotized, like everyone's just going through the motions. Even the kids... they don't seem excited for Christmas anymore."

Max leaned forward, his brow furrowed. "I've heard things. Weird things. People talking about Santa's magic—how it's not just a story anymore. Some say he's using his powers to control the town."

Lydia stared at him. "Santa? Using magic to control people? That sounds insane."

"I thought so too," Max said. "But there's something about this town, something that's been here for a long time. Ever since I was a kid, I've felt like there's something wrong with Windlake, something hidden beneath the surface. People come and go, but they always leave behind this... coldness."

Eva nodded. "I've heard rumors, too. Some people say that the magic of Christmas here is different. That it's not just about joy and giving. That it's about something far darker. Something that comes alive every year around Christmas."

Lydia shivered. "What do we do? How do we stop it?"

Max looked around at his friends. "We have to find out what's really going on. We have to go to the source."

They made their way to the heart of Windlake, where the giant Christmas tree stood in the square. The snow fell heavily around them, and the town felt so empty that it was almost suffocating. The lights on the tree twinkled in the otherwise silent night, casting long, eerie shadows across the square.

"I don't like this," Lydia said, her voice trembling. "It's so quiet. It's like we're not supposed to be here."

"We're getting closer," Max whispered. He led them toward the old church at the end of the square, a place they had never been before, even as children. Its doors were always locked, its windows dark. But tonight, they were open.

Inside, the air was thick with an unnatural stillness. The large stone walls were adorned with old Christmas decorations, cobwebs and dust clinging to them like forgotten memories. But what caught their attention was the figure standing at the front of the church, illuminated by a faint, flickering light.

It was Santa. But not the jolly figure they had grown up with. This Santa was tall, his face gaunt, his smile wide but twisted. His eyes gleamed with a malevolent glow, and his clothes were tattered, as if they had been worn for centuries. The red of his suit was stained dark, the fur trim soiled with age.

"You've come to see," he said, his voice deep and rasping. "To understand what Christmas truly means."

The group stood frozen, their bodies refusing to move.

"What is this?" Brian choked out. "What are you?"

Santa stepped forward, his grin widening. "I am the one who has given this town its spirit. I have controlled their belief, their joy. They think they celebrate Christmas, but they do not understand the cost. Every year, they give a piece of their soul to me, to the magic that I bring. But it is not magic of joy. It is the magic of control."

Lydia's heart sank. "You've been using Christmas to... control everyone?"

Santa nodded, his smile never faltering. "Every child who believes, every person who hopes, they are mine. They serve me. And now, you four—your minds are already mine, too. You have opened the door, and now you will never leave."

"No!" Lydia screamed. She turned to run, but her body wouldn't obey. Her legs were frozen, locked in place.

Max, Eva, and Brian's faces were pale, their eyes empty, as if they were no longer truly there. They had already been consumed. They had given in to the magic.

"You see," Santa continued, stepping closer, "Christmas is not about goodwill. It is not about warmth or joy. It is about power. And I, the true Santa, will rule this world as long as there are those who believe."

The darkness closed in, and Lydia felt herself slip into a void. Her mind, her body, her very soul were no longer hers. They had all become puppets of Satan's eternal scheme.

And as the church doors slammed shut behind them, the lesson was clear: belief can be a powerful force, but when it's twisted, it becomes the perfect tool for control. And when the magic fades, all that's left is darkness.

The Gift of Damnation

The Mallory family was like any other when it came to Christmas. The decorations went up in early December, the house was filled with the smell of gingerbread and pine, and they eagerly awaited the holiday's arrival. But there was one tradition that had set their Christmas apart from the others. For as long as anyone could remember, each year, without fail, they received a gift from Santa. A gift that, at first glance, seemed harmless, even thoughtful. But year after year, tragedy followed.

It started when Eleanor Mallory was a little girl. Her parents would wake up on Christmas morning to find an unmarked package sitting under the tree, wrapped in plain brown paper with no label, no note, just a ribbon tied around it. Inside would always be something that seemed appropriate for the year—a book, a small toy, a scarf—but something was always off. As she grew older, Eleanor began to notice a strange pattern. Every year, the gift would be followed by something dark. A broken bone, an illness, a death in the family. It was always something subtle, something that felt like a shadow creeping through their lives.

By the time Eleanor had children of her own, the tradition had continued. The gifts came each Christmas Eve, and each year, she would watch her own children—her son, Jack, and her daughter, Sarah—open their presents with innocent excitement, unaware of the curse that clung to every gift. The gifts seemed to grow more personal as the years passed. A small music box one year, a beautiful necklace the next. Gifts that seemed to hold meaning, like they were chosen specifically for the recipient. But with every gift came the same dreadful result: some tragedy would follow, something small but enough to keep the family on edge.

Eleanor tried to ignore it, tried to convince herself that it was just a coincidence. But she knew better. And this year, as she placed the unmarked package under the tree, the familiar chill crept up her spine. The house was full of life—the laughter of her children, the sound of the fire crackling in the hearth—but underneath it all, Eleanor could feel the weight of something watching, waiting.

The night before Christmas, Eleanor had a strange dream. She was a child again, standing in her parents' living room on Christmas Eve. The door to the kitchen was slightly ajar, and she could hear whispers, low and unintelligible, drifting from within. She approached, but when she reached for the doorknob, her mother appeared in the doorway, her eyes wide with fear. "You shouldn't be here," her mother whispered, a look of sheer terror on her face. "We can't escape it, Eleanor. We never could."

Eleanor woke with a start, her heart pounding. The dream was vivid, and it stayed with her throughout the day. But she couldn't allow herself to dwell on it. Not with the children so excited. Not with Christmas finally here.

When the morning came, Jack and Sarah rushed to the tree, their eyes wide with excitement. There, sitting at the foot of the tree, was the gift. Wrapped in the same brown paper, the same ribbon, the same eerie simplicity. Eleanor's stomach turned. She had always dreaded these moments, but this time felt different. This time, something inside her told her that this would be the year they uncovered the truth.

The children tore into the gift. Inside, they found a simple wooden box, exquisitely carved with intricate patterns. It looked like something from another time, old but somehow timeless. Jack's eyes lit up. "It's beautiful!" he exclaimed, running his fingers over the smooth surface. "What's inside, Mom?"

Eleanor opened the box carefully, her hands trembling. Inside, there was nothing but a small, folded piece of parchment. She unfolded it slowly, her eyes scanning the handwritten message:

"You are mine now. For all eternity."

A cold wave of dread washed over Eleanor as she read the words aloud. "What does this mean, Mom?" Jack asked, his voice trembling.

Eleanor couldn't speak. She could feel it—just as she had all those years ago. That strange, oppressive weight that had always lingered around Christmas. She stared at the box, feeling an overwhelming sense of wrongness emanating from it. Then, something clicked in her mind. The dream. The whispers. The warning from her mother.

She needed to know the truth. It was time to uncover the origins of this gift. As she had suspected, it wasn't just a simple tradition—it was a curse, one that had been passed down through generations.

Eleanor's investigation took her back to the town library, where she found old records and articles about Christmas in Windlake. She dug deeper into the town's history, piecing together bits of information that didn't seem to fit. And there, in the dustiest corner of the library, she discovered an old journal—one belonging to her great-grandmother, who had raised her mother.

The entries were cryptic, filled with half-formed thoughts, but one particular passage stood out:

"Every Christmas, the gift arrives. From the jolly man in the red suit. We believe it is Santa. But the truth is darker. He is not who they say he is. He is a demon, an agent of Satan, who uses the guise of Santa to bind the souls of the innocent. Every year, one gift. One soul claimed. There is no escape. We gave ourselves to him long ago."

Eleanor's hands shook as she read those words. The truth had been there all along, hidden in plain sight. The gifts weren't from Santa. They were from Satan himself. And every time her family accepted the gift, they were sealing their fate.

By the time she returned home, the realization had fully set in. The box—this year's gift—was not just a symbol of the season; it was a link, a chain binding her family to the infernal world. She had no time to warn Jack and Sarah. She heard them laughing downstairs, their voices filled with a joy that seemed so hollow now. The joy of Christmas was a lie. It had always been a lie.

She rushed to the living room, but as she entered, she froze. The box was gone. Jack and Sarah stood motionless in front of the fireplace, their eyes wide, fixed on something in the flames. The fire flickered and danced, but something was wrong. The warmth of the hearth had turned to ice. The children's eyes—those eyes—were empty, hollow, like they were no longer there.

"Mom?" Sarah's voice was distant, as if coming from far away.

Eleanor collapsed to her knees, understanding now that they had all been claimed, that their souls had already been taken.

The gift had been the final offering, and the truth was clear: every Christmas, the Mallory family had been bound to Satan's will, one gift at a time. And now, there was no escape. The final toll had been paid.

The Ho Ho Ho Curse

Lily had always loved Christmas. The twinkling lights, the warm scent of cinnamon and pine, the joy of unwrapping presents—everything about the holiday filled her with excitement. As a little girl, she would listen intently to the sound of sleigh bells jingling in the distance, imagining Santa's reindeer soaring across the snowy sky. But as she grew older, something began to change. Something that no one ever warned her about.

It started when she was nine, during the cold December nights leading up to Christmas. The first time she heard it, she was lying in bed, her room dimly lit by the soft glow of the Christmas tree. She had been drifting off to sleep when a sound broke through the quiet night. It was a laugh, familiar yet unsettling.

"Ho ho ho!" The deep, jolly voice echoed through the darkness outside her window. It was Santa, of course. But something was wrong. It didn't sound the way she remembered. It was too loud, too long, and too... sharp. Lily pulled the covers over her head, shivering despite the warmth of her room.

The next night, the laugh came again. Louder. Closer.

"Ho ho ho!"

Lily's heart raced, but she forced herself to remain still. It wasn't until the third night that she realized it was more than just a strange coincidence. The laugh was no longer jolly—it was menacing, deep and hollow, as though something sinister lurked behind it. She had heard enough horror stories about Christmas Eve—stories that whispered of evil forces hiding behind the merriment of the season—and now, her childhood sense of wonder was fading.

By the time she turned ten, the laugh had become a nightly occurrence. It echoed through the night with a steady rhythm, like a haunting chant, growing louder and more unsettling as the days passed. And then, one night, it changed.

"Ho ho hoooooo!" The laugh lasted longer than usual, stretching unnaturally, like a sound that had been twisted beyond recognition. Lily bolted upright in bed, her heart pounding. She could almost feel the darkness seeping into her room, pressing against her chest.

The next morning, she told her mother about the laugh. Her mother smiled gently, ruffling her hair.

"Don't worry, honey," she said in a soft voice. "It's just your imagination. Santa's laugh is always jolly, you know that."

But Lily wasn't convinced. She had started to notice other things—small, strange things. The shadows in her room seemed darker than usual. The air felt heavier, colder. And every time she closed her eyes, she could hear that laugh, echoing in her mind.

As the years went on, the laugh grew darker still. It was no longer just an unsettling sound—it was a presence, something that filled the room with an oppressive weight. When Lily turned eleven, she started feeling different. A strange energy filled her veins, something that made her more alert, more aware of things around her. At first, she thought it was just the inevitable changes that came with growing up. But the whispers began to grow louder. She would catch herself muttering the laugh under her breath, "Ho ho ho," and sometimes, she would even find herself smiling in a way that felt... wrong.

And then, on her twelfth Christmas Eve, Lily's world changed completely.

She was lying in bed, staring at the ceiling, when the laugh came again. But this time, it wasn't just a sound. It was a voice in her head, unmistakable and overwhelming.

"Ho ho ho... You are mine now."

Lily gasped, her body trembling with fear. She tried to sit up, but her limbs felt heavy, as though they were being weighed down by invisible hands. She fought to move, but it was no use. Her eyes darted around the room, but everything seemed to blur, her vision fading in and out as if reality itself was unraveling.

The laugh grew louder, more insistent, until it felt as if the walls themselves were shaking. And then, she saw it—a figure in the corner of her room, tall and dark, wearing the tattered remnants of a Santa suit. Its eyes glowed with an unnatural red light, and its smile—oh, its smile—was twisted, an abomination of the jolly old man she had once adored.

"Santa," she whispered, her voice shaking.

The figure stepped forward, its presence suffocating, filling every corner of her room with an overwhelming darkness. "No," it said, its voice gravelly, ancient. "I am not Santa. I am the one who has claimed your soul. You belong to me now."

Lily's heart pounded in her chest as she realized the truth. The laugh, the magic—it had never been a blessing. It was a curse, one that had been cast upon her long ago, a spell that bound her to something far darker than she had ever imagined. Every year, with every laugh, she had unknowingly given her soul over to Satan, feeding his power. And now, it was too late to break free.

"You are mine," the figure repeated, its voice like a drumbeat in her head. "You and your family. All of you have been chosen. You are my minions now, for all eternity."

Lily wanted to scream, to run, but she couldn't move. Her body no longer obeyed her. She could feel the coldness of the room seeping into her bones, the darkness wrapping around her, claiming her, as the figure's grin widened impossibly wide.

The figure leaned in close, its breath cold against her ear. "You will never escape. You are mine, Lily. You are all mine."

And as the darkness consumed her, she understood. The laugh, the gift, the magic—it had never been about joy. It had always been a lie. A trap. Santa was never the jolly, benevolent figure of childhood tales. He was a tool of Satan, a vessel through which souls were harvested, one laugh at a time. And now, Lily was a part of it, her fate sealed, just as the others before her had been.

The last thing she heard was the laugh. Not the warm, jolly sound of Christmas, but a cruel, mocking, evil laugh that echoed in her mind for eternity.

"Ho ho ho... You belong to me."

Under the Mistletoe

The Miller family had always celebrated Christmas with a quiet, comforting tradition: the mistletoe. It hung above the doorway in their living room, its green leaves and white berries a reminder of the old holiday customs, a symbol of goodwill and love. For years, they'd followed the simple tradition of stealing a kiss whenever someone stood beneath it, laughing together at the mild awkwardness and playfulness of it all. But this year, as Christmas approached, something about the mistletoe seemed different. It felt heavier, as if it were watching them, waiting for them to acknowledge something they had long ignored.

Alice Miller, the matriarch of the family, noticed it first. Her eyes flickered toward the mistletoe, and she felt a slight tremor run down her spine. It was Christmas Eve, and as she stood in the kitchen preparing the holiday dinner, the laughter of her children, Megan and Jake, filled the house. They were setting up the tree in the living room, stringing lights and placing ornaments. Everything seemed perfect, just as it had in years past, but there was a tension in the air, a tightness in her chest that made her uneasy.

Later that evening, as the family gathered around the table for dinner, they shared stories of Christmases gone by, exchanging small gifts and memories. The mistletoe hung silently above the doorway, its berries glistening in the dim light. After the meal, as the evening stretched on, Jake, now a teenager, teasingly stood beneath it and looked at Megan.

"Come on, Meg. You're not too old for a kiss, right?"

Megan rolled her eyes but smiled. "I guess not," she said with a laugh, stepping forward. As she kissed Jake on the cheek, something strange happened. There was a faint, almost imperceptible shift in the air, like the room had grown a few degrees colder. The atmosphere felt dense, charged with a presence Alice couldn't quite place.

She shook it off, attributing the sensation to the old house settling or perhaps the strange weather outside. But then, as her eyes wandered back to the mistletoe, she felt the same unsettling chill. It seemed to pulse, as if it were alive, its berries glowing faintly.

Later, as the night wore on, Alice found herself alone in the hallway, passing under the mistletoe herself. Without thinking, she leaned in and kissed her husband, John, on the cheek. A small gesture, a habit she had done countless times. But the moment her lips touched his skin, she felt a sharp jolt of electricity run through her body. Her eyes widened, and she pulled away quickly. John didn't seem to notice, but Alice was shaken, her heartbeat erratic, her breath shallow.

The laughter from the living room sounded distant, muffled. She stumbled back into the living room, her eyes instinctively drawn back to the mistletoe. Her mind raced as she tried to shake the growing sense of dread. Something was wrong. She had no explanation for it, but she knew with a sickening certainty that the mistletoe, the innocent plant that had always been part of their holiday tradition, was no longer just a harmless decoration.

That night, when the family went to bed, Alice lay awake in the dark, staring at the ceiling, unable to shake the strange feeling that had taken hold of her. A few hours later, she was jolted awake by a sound—a soft, almost imperceptible whisper that came from the direction of the living room. She sat up in bed, heart racing, trying to make sense of it. There was something in the air, a whisper, a presence that lingered just beyond the edge of her consciousness.

Her breath caught in her throat as she saw a shadow move at the edge of the doorway. She jumped to her feet and hurried to the living room, half-expecting to find someone there. But the room was empty, save for the mistletoe hanging above the door.

And then she saw it.

The mistletoe was no longer simply a holiday decoration. It had grown larger, its tendrils twisting unnaturally, and its berries glowed with an eerie red hue. Alice felt her legs buckle beneath her as a low, guttural laugh echoed through the room—one that sent a chill of terror down her spine. It was a laugh she knew all too well, the one that echoed in her nightmares.

"Ho ho ho..." the voice rumbled, distorted and chilling.

Alice's heart pounded in her chest as she backed away from the mistletoe, the laugh growing louder, more sinister. She turned and ran to the kitchen, where she found John, still sleeping soundly, unaware of the growing terror. Her hand trembled as she reached for the phone to call for help, but something held her back.

The laughter filled the house again, this time louder, more forceful. "You are mine now," the voice echoed. "Your souls belong to me."

Suddenly, she understood. It wasn't just a harmless tradition. The mistletoe had been a portal, a gateway for something darker than she had ever imagined. Each kiss under it, each act of affection, had been a thread in an unholy ritual. The innocuous plant had been used to slowly draw her family into Satan's grasp. Each kiss had tied their souls further to the darkness.

She ran to the living room, where she saw John and the children standing, their eyes glazed, their faces frozen in a haunting smile. "No!" Alice screamed, her voice cracking. "Get away from it!"

But they didn't move. Their bodies were no longer their own. As she stood there, paralyzed with fear, she realized the truth: the mistletoe had done its work. Each kiss had allowed a piece of their soul to be claimed. They were no longer her family. They were vessels, puppets bound to serve Satan for eternity.

Alice turned and fled into the night, but as she did, she heard the laughter follow her, a cold, mocking sound that filled the world with despair.

And in the end, she understood: there are no innocent traditions. Behind every gift, behind every act of goodwill, lies a darker force waiting for the right moment to claim what it has been promised.

The mistletoe, once a symbol of love, had turned into a gateway to damnation. And in the cold, silent night, Alice realized she was already too late. The curse had claimed her, just as it had claimed them all.

The Christmas Wraith

It was the second Christmas since Michael's wife, Anne, had passed. Her sudden death, just days before the holiday, had shattered his world. For a long time, he couldn't bring himself to even acknowledge Christmas. But this year, he decided to make the effort. For his children, at least. They were small, too young to understand fully, but old enough to feel the absence. The lights on the tree, the stockings hung by the fire—they needed something normal in their lives, something to hold on to. So, against his better judgment, he carried on.

It was Christmas Eve when Michael first heard the whispers. He had put the children to bed, settled by the fire, and tried to relax with a glass of wine, though his mind was anything but at ease. His thoughts kept drifting to Anne—what she would have said, what she would have done. Would she have loved the tree this year? Would she have laughed at his half-hearted attempts to make the holiday joyful?

The fire crackled, the warmth of it doing little to ease the cold knot in his chest. Then came the sound—soft at first, like a rustling in the corner of the room. Michael paused, trying to shake the creeping unease. He was alone, and yet it felt as if the room was filled with something else—something dark, something ancient.

Suddenly, the air grew heavier, colder. He shivered, rising to check the windows for drafts. As he walked across the room, the low whispering grew louder, just out of reach, as if it were coming from the walls themselves. It wasn't a voice, not exactly. More like a hum, a chorus of murmurs. And then he heard it.

"Ho ho ho..."

The deep laugh sent a jolt through him. Michael spun around, his breath catching in his throat. The room was empty. The fire flickered, casting long shadows, but there was no one there.

But that laugh... it wasn't right. It wasn't jolly. It was cold, hollow, as if something were mocking the very idea of joy. It didn't belong here.

He shook his head, trying to dismiss it. He was exhausted, and the grief was doing strange things to his mind. The children were safe in their rooms; he was alone in the house, in a place that was still too full of memories.

Then, there was a knock at the door.

Michael froze. No one ever came by this late. Not on Christmas Eve. He glanced at the clock—past midnight now. Who could it be?

When he opened the door, there was no one there, just the cold, empty street covered in snow. The only sign of life was the fresh imprint of footsteps, but they led away from his house, not toward it.

A chill ran down his spine. It wasn't just the cold night air. There was something wrong about all of this, something beyond the grief that still haunted him.

He stepped back inside, closing the door, but then he heard it again. This time, closer. That same mocking laugh.

"Ho ho ho..."

It was coming from the hallway, from the kitchen.

His heart pounded in his chest as he moved cautiously through the dark house, his steps muffled by the thick carpet. He reached the kitchen, and there, in the corner of the room, stood a figure—a silhouette in the dim light of the hallway. At first, he thought it was a trick of the light, but as his eyes adjusted, the figure became clearer.

It was tall, wearing a suit of red and white, a large sack slung over its shoulder. But it was not the jolly Santa Claus Michael remembered from childhood. This figure was gaunt, its skin pale and stretched thin, like it had not seen daylight in decades. Its eyes were black voids, hollow and endless. And its grin—its grin was wide, far too wide, splitting the face in an unnatural way. It was the kind of smile that filled you with a deep, suffocating dread.

Michael's breath caught in his throat. "Who are you?" he managed to choke out.

The figure tilted its head, the grin growing even wider, as if amused by his fear.

"Ho ho ho," it repeated, its voice distorted, more raspy than jovial. "The time has come."

Michael took a step back, his mind racing, panic overtaking his senses. He wanted to run, but his body refused to move. The figure slowly advanced, its steps deliberate, its eyes never leaving Michael's.

"You think Christmas is about gifts, about joy. You think Santa brings magic," the figure whispered, its voice chillingly cold. "But Christmas is not what you believe. It is a harvest. A time for the wraiths to gather. Every year, one soul is taken. And this year, it is yours."

Michael stumbled backward, the words sinking in. Soul taken? What was it talking about? He wanted to scream, but no sound came out. His legs felt like stone.

"Every year," the figure continued, "Santa does not bring gifts. He collects them. Those who celebrate Christmas give their joy, their energy, and in return, he takes what belongs to him."

The figure reached into the sack it carried, pulling out a small, blackened ornament. It was strange—shaped like a twisted, dark version of a Christmas tree, its edges sharp, its surface crawling with faint, otherworldly symbols.

"This," the figure said, holding it up, "is the final gift. You were always meant to receive it. Now, your soul belongs to me."

Michael tried to move, tried to scream, but it was as though his body was frozen in place. He could feel it—the weight of the figure's presence, the suffocating energy in the room. He was trapped. Trapped by something ancient, something he had never believed in.

"Every Christmas," the figure continued, "I come to harvest. You are the sacrifice. Your life force will fuel the magic, and with each year, it grows stronger. Your joy, your Christmas cheer, are nothing more than fuel for my master."

And then, the figure reached out, its hand cold as death, and touched the ornament to Michael's chest.

There was a flash of light, an unbearable burning sensation, and then... nothing.

When Michael woke, he was standing in the living room again, the clock on the wall showing the same time it had when the figure appeared. The house was silent, eerily still. The figure was gone. But as he glanced toward the tree, he saw something that froze him in place—his children's faces, hollow and lifeless, staring back at him from the shadows.

They were no longer his children. They, too, had been claimed.

Michael's breath caught in his throat as he realized the true horror of what had happened. He had become a puppet of the wraith, just as everyone before him had. Christmas wasn't a time of magic, of joy. It was a time for death—a time for the wraith to feast on the lives of those foolish enough to believe.

And now, Michael understood: belief was not a gift—it was the curse.

The Eternal Winter

The first snow had come early, too early. The people of Ashbrook were used to cold winters, but the snowflakes that began to fall in late October were thick and heavy, as if the sky itself was weeping. The townspeople were confused at first, but as the weeks passed, they realized this wasn't just an unusually early winter. It was a permanent one.

By mid-November, the first signs of panic started to spread. The snow didn't stop. It blanketed the town, piling higher and higher, covering windows, doors, streets, and rooftops. And with it came an unnatural chill that settled deep into the bones of anyone who ventured outside. The Christmas lights that were hung up early in an attempt to bring cheer flickered and dimmed under the weight of the cold, as though the holiday spirit was being slowly drained from the town.

"Something's wrong," whispered Emma, a sharp-eyed fourteen-year-old girl who had lived in Ashbrook her entire life. She was sitting in the dimly lit corner of the local library with her two friends, Josh and Sarah, pouring over old books. They had all felt the strange, oppressive weight of the endless winter, the heaviness in the air that no one could explain.

"This isn't just weather," Josh said, his voice low. "This is something... unnatural."

"It's like the season is stuck," Sarah added, her fingers absently twirling a lock of her hair. "It doesn't feel like Christmas. It feels like... death."

Emma stared out the frosted window, her breath fogging up the glass. "We need to find out what's causing this. We can't keep going like this."

The town had become increasingly isolated. The snow piled up so high that the roads were impassable, and even the local school had shut down due to the cold. The people of Ashbrook huddled inside their homes, trying to stay warm, but the cold seeped in no matter what they did.

Late one night, Emma couldn't sleep. Her mind raced with thoughts of the endless winter. She had overheard her parents talking about strange occurrences in the woods, but they quickly hushed their voices whenever she entered the room. That curiosity, that burning need to know the truth, drove her to slip out of bed and sneak out of the house.

The snow crunched beneath her boots as she made her way through the dark streets of Ashbrook. The town was eerily silent, its buildings covered in layers of snow like monuments to forgotten times. As she passed the town square, her heart skipped a beat. There, in the center of the square, was a figure standing beneath the only remaining light. It was tall, cloaked in a red suit, and his face was obscured by the dark shadow of a hood. He seemed to radiate a coldness that made the air even more frigid.

Emma's breath caught in her throat as she approached the figure. The chill in the air was unbearable, as if the very essence of winter had taken shape before her. And then, she heard it—an unmistakable laugh, low and guttural, but unmistakably familiar.

"Ho ho ho..."

The laugh echoed through the empty streets, chilling Emma to her core. She stepped forward, her feet moving of their own accord, drawn to the figure. The laugh sounded wrong, so wrong. It wasn't the jovial chuckle she remembered from childhood. It was dark, hollow, and full of malice.

"Who are you?" Emma asked, her voice trembling despite her attempt at courage.

The figure turned slowly, his eyes glowing red from beneath the shadow of his hood. Emma's blood ran cold as she recognized him—Santa Claus, or what had once been Santa. His face was a grotesque mockery of the old man she had known, his smile stretched too wide, his skin gray and mottled. His eyes were not kind, but empty, hollow pits of blackness.

"I am the keeper of the frost," he said, his voice low, as if the words were a secret only meant for her. "And you, Emma, are the next to understand the truth."

Emma's heart raced as she took a step back, but the figure raised a hand, and a gust of cold wind slammed into her, forcing her to remain where she stood.

"This winter," Santa continued, "is no accident. It is a curse, a spell that I cast to prepare the world for what is to come. The old magic that once filled Christmas with joy now serves a darker purpose. The cold that spreads across this town is but the beginning."

Emma's mind reeled, struggling to grasp what was happening. "What do you mean? What is this about? Why is the town freezing?"

"The season of Christmas is not just a time of giving," Santa said, his voice deepening with each word. "It is a time for collecting. Every year, when children believe in me, their faith feeds the magic. But that magic—my magic—belongs to something far darker, something far older. I am not just Santa Claus. I am the wraith of winter, the herald of the eternal cold. And every Christmas, I take more souls, binding them to my master."

Emma's breath caught in her throat. "What do you mean, taking souls? Who's your master?"

Santa's grin widened, revealing sharp, yellowed teeth. "My master is the one who rules this world through fear and despair. He waits in the shadows, and with each passing year, as belief in Christmas grows stronger, so does his power. The endless winter you feel is merely a taste of what is to come. Soon, the world will freeze, its warmth drained forever. The people will fall into darkness, and Satan will reign."

A sickening realization hit Emma like a physical blow. Santa—the jolly, beloved figure—was nothing more than a servant, a wraith who used Christmas to harvest the souls of the innocent, feeding Satan's reign over the world.

"And you," Santa said, his voice dropping to a whisper, "will soon be one of us."

Emma stumbled back, but the figure stepped forward, his hand reaching out to her. The cold was unbearable, wrapping around her like an icy vice. She tried to scream, but no sound came out.

And then, as she felt the darkness closing in, she understood—there was no escape. The winter had come, not as a simple storm, but as a curse, a tool for Satan's dominion. The belief in Santa had been nothing more than a ruse, a way to bind humanity to the frozen grip of Hell itself.

Emma's final thought, before the cold consumed her completely, was that the world would never be the same again. Christmas had become a tool of destruction, and all of them—everyone who had ever believed—were now bound to the wraith, trapped in eternal winter, forever.

The Secret of the North Pole

For years, Nathaniel West had been a journalist driven by the truth, no matter how dark or uncomfortable it might be. His career had been built on uncovering secrets, exposing corruption, and chasing stories that others were too afraid to touch. But when the assignment came through—an investigation into the truth behind the legend of Santa Claus—he didn't expect it would lead him to a place darker than anything he'd encountered before.

The letter had come one cold December afternoon. An anonymous source had tipped him off, claiming that the stories of Santa's workshop were far from what the public believed. Instead of the jolly, gift-giving figure loved by children across the world, Santa was a terrifying force, ruling over the North Pole like a king over a kingdom of suffering. The letter offered no further details, only a cryptic invitation: *Come to the North Pole. The truth awaits.*

Nathaniel's initial reaction had been skepticism. It was a hoax, he told himself. A desperate grab for attention, or maybe a sick joke. But then the stories started to pile up. The whispers among locals in remote northern communities. The sudden disappearance of individuals who had ventured too close to the Arctic. And the strange pattern of disappearances around Christmas time.

His curiosity won out. Armed with nothing more than his notebook and camera, Nathaniel booked a flight, heading toward the edge of the world. As the plane flew over the frozen tundra, he couldn't shake the feeling that he was heading into something far deeper than a simple investigation. The air seemed unnaturally still, the vast white plains below the plane stretching endlessly, as though the earth itself was holding its breath.

When he arrived at a small town near the Arctic Circle, he found little more than a few weathered buildings and a handful of residents who avoided his questions. But there was one man, an older gentleman named Simon, who seemed to know more than he let on. The man had eyes that spoke of a life lived in constant fear, and when Nathaniel asked about the North Pole, Simon grew visibly agitated.

"It's not what you think," Simon said, his voice trembling. "You should turn back. You don't know what you're walking into. The North Pole isn't a magical land. It's a fortress. A prison."

Nathaniel pushed further, sensing something deeper beneath Simon's warnings. "What do you mean? What's really up there?"

Simon hesitated, glancing nervously around. "Santa's workshop isn't a place of joy. It's a breeding ground... for demons. The man in the red suit isn't what you think he is. You've heard the legends of the jolly old man, right? The one who gives gifts? But what they don't tell you is that every year, as he delivers those gifts, he's also harvesting souls. The workshop isn't making toys. It's making servants—creatures born of hell itself. It's not a place of magic, it's a place of power. Dark power."

Simon's face was ashen as he spoke, his hands trembling. "People who go there don't come back. Or if they do, they're not the same."

The words sent a chill down Nathaniel's spine. He tried to press Simon further, but the old man had already turned away, muttering something about the 'darkness that would claim him.' Nathaniel, frustrated but undeterred, booked a guide and set off toward the North Pole the very next day.

The journey was grueling. The further north they went, the more oppressive the atmosphere became. The sun barely rose above the horizon, casting an eerie, low light over the endless expanse of snow and ice. There were no animals, no signs of life—only the crunch of their boots in the snow and the sound of the wind howling through the desolate wilderness.

As they reached the base of a towering ice mountain, Nathaniel's guide suddenly stopped, looking over his shoulder with wide, terrified eyes.

"I can't take you further," he said, voice shaking. "No one goes up there. No one comes back."

But Nathaniel, driven by his need to know, continued alone. He hiked up the frozen slope, exhaustion weighing heavily on his body. The air grew thinner, colder, and just when he thought he might collapse, he saw it. A dark, looming structure in the distance—a fortress of black ice and steel that seemed to rise from the ground like a twisted monument to despair. The windows were dark, but faint, unnatural lights flickered inside.

The door creaked open as if it had been expecting him. He stepped inside, his breath catching in his throat at what he saw.

The interior was nothing like the stories. There were no elves, no joyful workers—just rows and rows of twisted, deformed figures hunched over mechanical contraptions, their faces empty, their eyes hollow. They worked tirelessly, assembling what looked like grotesque toys, but upon closer inspection, Nathaniel saw that these were not toys at all. They were creatures—demonic figures, half human, half machine, bound by chains of fire and ice.

A low, guttural laugh echoed through the walls.

"Ho ho ho," the voice boomed, but it wasn't jolly. It was cold, like the sound of a predator stalking its prey.

Nathaniel turned and saw him—the man who had once been Santa. But there was nothing jolly about him now. His eyes were black as pits, his face gaunt, skin stretched tightly over his bones. His smile was not friendly, but twisted, stretching impossibly wide. The red suit he wore was soaked in something dark, something that looked like blood.

"You've come to uncover the truth," the figure said, his voice deep and raspy. "But now, you will become part of it."

Nathaniel tried to run, but his body wouldn't move. The air seemed to freeze around him, his limbs heavy, as though the very essence of the place was pulling him into its grip.

"You wanted to know what Christmas really is, didn't you?" The figure's smile widened further. "Christmas is not about giving. It is about control. Each year, I harvest souls, feed my power, and create more servants. You, like all others before you, will be one of them. The North Pole is not a place of wonder—it is a prison, a hellish breeding ground. And now, you belong to me."

Nathaniel struggled against the invisible chains that bound him, but it was useless. The cold seeped into his bones as the figure approached. And then, everything went dark.

When he awoke, he was no longer alone. The workshop was silent, save for the sound of heavy breathing. Around him stood the creatures—the half-human, half-demonic beings, their hollow eyes staring at him. He understood then. He had become one of them.

And as the cursed workshop continued to churn out horrors for Satan, Nathaniel's soul became another thread in the tapestry of despair. He was bound to the fortress, to the wraith that had once been Santa, forevermore.

The truth, the dark truth, was that Christmas was never meant for joy. It had always been a time for harvest.

Satan's Army of Elves

Christmas had always been Alice's favorite time of year. The decorations, the music, the warmth of family gathered around the tree—it was a fleeting moment of joy in an otherwise difficult life. But that Christmas felt different. Something was off, something she couldn't quite put her finger on. The air was thick with an unease that she hadn't noticed before, a quiet fear that seemed to linger just beneath the surface of all the holiday cheer.

It started with little things. The way the neighborhood children had grown quiet, their faces more hollow than they should have been. The way they seemed to look past her, as if they couldn't see her at all. Alice chalked it up to the stress of the season, the relentless expectations placed on everyone to be merry. But when her son, Tommy, asked her about the "elves" in their backyard, she felt the first tremor of something wrong.

"Mom, the elves are watching me again," he said one evening, his voice shaking. "They're in the garden, behind the trees. They smile when I look at them, but they don't look like the ones in the stories. They're different."

Alice brushed it off as a child's imagination, though the look in Tommy's eyes made her pause. The following morning, Tommy refused to go outside. He sat in his room, his small hands clutching a stuffed bear tightly to his chest. He wouldn't speak much, only muttering things about "the elves" and how they "wanted to take him."

When Alice went to check the garden, she saw nothing out of the ordinary. Just the bare branches of winter, the wind stirring the dead leaves. But as she turned back toward the house, she noticed something strange—something in the corner of her vision, a fleeting glimpse of small figures darting between the trees. Her heart pounded in her chest as the hairs on the back of her neck stood up.

That night, after Tommy had fallen asleep, Alice went to check the Christmas presents under the tree. They were all perfectly wrapped, just as they had been that morning. But something was wrong. The air felt colder around them, and as she reached for one of the gifts, she heard a faint, dissonant laugh—a sharp, jarring sound that made her blood run cold.

Her hands trembled as she held the gift, and in that moment, she knew. There was no joy in these presents, no love. They were traps.

Alice tore open the wrapping paper, revealing a small wooden toy, intricately carved and painted in bright colors. It was beautiful in an unsettling way, the craftsmanship perfect—but as her fingers brushed the surface, the toy seemed to come alive. It twitched, and the eyes painted onto it flickered with a malevolent glint. The wooden figure smiled, but the smile was wrong. It was a grin of twisted malice, as though it knew something Alice did not. Something she was beginning to dread.

She had to protect Tommy. She had to get rid of the gifts.

Her heart pounded as she ran to Tommy's room, but when she opened the door, she froze. There, standing at the foot of his bed, were the elves—small, grotesque creatures with sharp teeth and hollow eyes, their features stretched in unnatural grins. They were watching her son sleep, their hands outstretched as though they were waiting for the perfect moment to claim him.

The room seemed to close in on Alice. Her legs felt weak, her breath shallow, as if the very air had thickened with a dark presence. The elves weren't what she had imagined. They weren't the cheerful, mischievous figures from stories. No, these creatures were something far darker. Their faces were gaunt, their eyes sunken and empty, and their skin was pale, like dead flesh, stretched tight over their bones. They weren't toys, they weren't helpers—they were demons, their twisted forms a mockery of innocence.

The largest elf turned toward Alice, its smile widening, and she knew—knew without a doubt—that they had been waiting for this moment. Waiting for her to discover the truth.

"They're not gifts," the elf hissed in a voice that sent chills down her spine. "They're chains. Each present, each toy, is a trap to bind your child to the dark lord. We take them, and their souls belong to him."

Alice stumbled backward, her mind racing. This wasn't just a fantasy. This was real. The toys. The elves. The entire tradition of Christmas—it was all part of a plan to harvest children's souls, to bind them to Satan's will. The gifts weren't about giving; they were about taking. The more children believed, the more power Satan gained, and the elves were the instruments of that power, working to claim the innocent.

"No," Alice whispered, her voice shaking. "No, I won't let you take him."

But the elf only laughed, the sound like nails scraping across glass. "You already lost him the moment you accepted the gifts. Every toy, every story—it's all part of the ritual. The children are marked the moment they believe. They're already ours."

Alice's heart clenched in fear. She turned to Tommy, but he was no longer the same. His eyes, once bright and full of life, were dull, lifeless. He was staring up at the elves, his expression vacant, as if he were already lost to them.

"Tommy, no," Alice cried, rushing to him, but it was too late. The elves stepped forward, their hands reaching for him, and Tommy did not resist. He smiled, a slow, twisted grin spreading across his face as the creatures began to encircle him.

The darkness closed in, and Alice felt a cold, crushing weight on her chest. She was too late. There was no saving him now. Tommy was already claimed, and the elves were taking him, body and soul, into the abyss.

As they disappeared into the shadows, leaving Alice standing alone in the cold, empty room, the sound of a distant laugh echoed in her ears—Santa's laugh. And for the first time, Alice understood the true meaning of Christmas. It was never about giving, never about joy. It had always been about taking—about feeding the darkness.

And Alice, helpless in the face of it, realized too late that she had been part of the ritual all along. The elves hadn't just come for Tommy. They had come for all of them.

The Devil's Gifts

It was Christmas Eve, and the air outside was frigid, the streets slick with fresh snow. Inside the house, the scent of pine and cinnamon filled the air as the warm glow from the fireplace bathed the room in a cozy light. Henry sat on the floor, eagerly tearing through the wrapping paper of his Christmas presents. He was twelve years old, old enough to have grown skeptical of Santa Claus, yet still too young to shake the childlike wonder that came with the holiday.

His parents had worked hard this year, and it showed in the stack of gifts that sat before him. He had always been the kind of boy who loved presents, the shiny paper, the ribbons, the bows. But tonight, as he unwrapped each gift, a strange feeling crept over him. It wasn't just the excitement that bubbled inside him—it was something else, something darker. A sensation of being drawn in, as though the gifts themselves were pulling him deeper into a world he didn't understand.

The first gift was a small wooden soldier, intricately carved with a stoic face. It was a fine piece of craftsmanship, but when Henry touched it, the soldier's painted eyes seemed to flicker, almost as if they were alive. He laughed it off at first, but then the toy began to twitch in his hands. The soldier's tiny wooden feet moved, and it turned its head toward him with a sharp, sudden motion. Henry dropped it in alarm, but when he looked again, the toy had returned to its original position, perfectly still.

He quickly moved on to the next gift, a bright red ball. A simple gift, but when he bounced it on the floor, it didn't just rebound—it rolled across the room, stopping perfectly at the foot of the tree. That wasn't normal. It wasn't possible. But before he could voice his concerns, the next gift caught his eye—a small metal compass, with a brass needle that twitched nervously, pointing somewhere just beyond his reach. His heart pounded as he watched the needle turn in sharp, erratic movements, as though it were alive and searching for something.

Confused, Henry turned to his parents, who were sitting at the table, lost in their conversation, unaware of his growing unease. They seemed so... distant. So detached from the gifts, from him. His mother smiled at him, but her smile didn't reach her eyes. His father, sitting across from her, appeared distracted, his face pale and drawn, as if something had drained him of life.

Henry, unable to shake the feeling that something was wrong, took the compass in his hand, and that's when it happened—the sudden shift. The lights in the room flickered once, then dimmed, as a chill filled the air. His parents were no longer smiling. Their faces were frozen in expressionless stares, as if they had been turned to stone.

The world around him seemed to warp and twist, and the warmth from the fire seemed to shrink away, replaced by a cold, suffocating darkness. The toys, now scattered across the floor, began to move of their own accord, crawling toward him like predatory animals. The soldier marched in perfect step toward his feet. The ball bounced itself toward him, rolling faster, faster. The compass needle spun wildly, as if seeking to cut through the fabric of reality itself.

And then, there was a voice.

It was faint at first, a whisper in the back of his mind. It called his name, soft and smooth like silk. He tried to ignore it, but the voice grew louder, more insistent, as if it were coming from within him. His heart raced, and his fingers tightened around the compass, as though it was pulling him in, compelling him to listen.

"Henry..."

The whisper seemed to seep from the walls themselves, curling through his thoughts. He fought to push it away, but the voice only grew stronger, wrapping around his mind like a vine, tightening, squeezing. The room began to tilt, the shadows thickening, spreading like ink in water. And then, there in the darkness, he saw it—a figure in the doorway, tall and imposing, draped in a cloak of deepest black. His eyes burned with an unnatural red glow, and the smile on his face was twisted and malevolent.

Henry's breath caught in his throat as he recognized the figure. It was Santa, but not the Santa from the stories. This Santa was different—his face was gaunt, his skin pale and stretched tight over his skull. His grin was wide, impossibly wide, exposing sharp teeth that gleamed in the dark.

"You've been chosen, Henry," the voice rumbled, the whisper now a deep, resonant growl that seemed to shake the floor beneath him. *"Chosen to receive the greatest gift of all. The gift of power. The gift of control. The gift of damnation."*

The toys around him continued to move, their eyes now glowing with the same red hue as the figure in the doorway. The soldier, the ball, the compass—all of them were his servants, moving at his command.

"W-What do you mean?" Henry stammered, his voice shaking as he clutched the compass tighter. "What's happening? What do you want from me?"

The figure took a step forward, its grin widening as it approached him.

"You've already given me your soul, Henry. You just didn't know it. Every year, children like you open my gifts, and each gift seals their fate. Each toy is a piece of me, a part of my power that you welcome into your world. And now, you belong to me. You always have."

The room spun, and Henry stumbled back, falling to the floor as the realization hit him like a wave. Each toy, each gift—it wasn't about joy. It wasn't about love. It was a trap, a chain binding him to a dark destiny he had never understood.

He tried to fight it, to pull away, but the power of the toys was too strong. The compass's needle dug into his palm, and the soldier's wooden feet began to march again, step by step toward him. Henry felt his body grow cold, his heart slow as the gifts twisted their power into his flesh, claiming him, body and soul.

The last thing he saw before the darkness overtook him was the red glow in Santa's eyes and the horrible, knowing grin that stretched across his face.

And then Henry knew the truth—the Devil's gifts had never been gifts at all. They were chains. And now, he wore them forever.

The Last Christmas

It had been three years since Christmas had become something more than just a holiday. The air was thick with the scent of pine, and the world was always covered in a blanket of snow. But there was no joy in the air. No cheer. Just an oppressive silence that hung over everything, as if the very earth itself was waiting for something. The world had become a place of endless winter, where Santa wasn't a jolly old man, but a tyrant whose eyes burned with the infernal heat of Hell.

The people had tried to resist, once. A small group of rebels, scattered across the world, had fought back against the growing influence of Santa and his dark empire. They had seen the signs: the way every Christmas seemed to stretch on forever, how the gifts that arrived at their doorsteps were never quite right, how the children who once believed were now brainwashed, their eyes vacant, their spirits dimmed. Those who resisted were silenced, their homes torn apart, their families erased from existence. But the rebels had never stopped fighting.

Emma was one of the last. A member of the Resistance, she had spent the last two years hiding, moving from safe house to safe house, never staying in one place for too long. Santa's agents—those who had fallen under his sway—were always hunting, always watching. But Emma wasn't like the others. She had a purpose, a mission, a truth she had to share. A truth that would either save or doom them all.

She met with the others under the cover of darkness, in a forgotten underground bunker that smelled of damp earth and stale air. The Resistance had learned much in the years they had fought, uncovering pieces of Santa's true nature, the nature that the world had long forgotten. Santa wasn't just a magical being who brought joy to children—he was something far darker. Something ancient.

"Emma, you look tired," said Adam, the leader of their small faction, his face etched with weariness. He had been at this for far too long. They all had. But they couldn't stop now.

"I'm fine," Emma replied, her voice hoarse. "I've seen something—something terrible. We're running out of time."

Adam raised an eyebrow. "What do you mean?"

Emma's fingers clenched into fists. "I found it. The truth. The origins of Santa's power. The last piece we've been missing."

They all leaned in, their eyes darkened by the weight of their collective burden. Emma pulled out an old book, worn and tattered, the pages yellowed with age. It had been passed down through generations of rebels, each one hoping to find the key to stopping Santa. But the truth had always eluded them.

"Santa isn't what we thought," Emma said, her voice shaking with disbelief. "He's not just a demon. He's the Devil himself. And he's not here to deliver gifts. He's here to conquer. The entire world is his kingdom now, and Christmas is his domain."

The room fell silent. The others exchanged glances, as if unsure whether to believe her. But Emma continued, her voice growing more urgent with every word.

"I found the ritual, the one that bound him to Earth. It's tied to Christmas, to the Winter Solstice. Every year, the world grows colder, darker, and Santa's power grows stronger. He's not giving gifts; he's taking souls, one by one, turning the children into his army. He feeds off the belief, the hope, the joy. But it's not for us—it's for him. And now, he's preparing for the final stage. The last Christmas. The one where he will fully take control."

There was a long pause, and then Sarah, the youngest of the group, spoke. "So what do we do? How do we stop him?"

Emma shook her head. "We can't stop him. It's already too late. The rituals are complete. There's no reversing it. Every year, he grows stronger. And now, we're about to enter the final phase."

Adam slammed his fist on the table. "But we've been fighting for so long. There has to be something—some way to stop him!"

Emma's eyes softened. She knew what he was thinking. They all wanted a way out. A way to save the world. But the truth was hard to swallow, harder than any of them could have prepared for.

"There is no way out," Emma said, her voice barely a whisper. "The end has already been written. We were never meant to stop it. We were never meant to win."

The others stared at her in stunned silence, as if they couldn't believe the words that had just left her mouth. It felt like a death sentence, and in a way, it was. But Emma had known this truth for a long time, ever since she'd first discovered the ancient texts, the ones that detailed the rise of Santa, the true nature of his power.

And now, it was too late to change the course of history.

"Christmas was always a trap," Emma continued. "A holiday designed to enslave us. To make us believe in something that was never real, to give our spirits over willingly. Each year, we celebrated it, and each year, we gave him more power."

"Then why fight?" Adam demanded, his face red with anger. "Why have we been sacrificing so much, if it was all for nothing?"

Emma looked down at the book in her hands, her fingers tracing the edges of the worn pages. She had the truth now, but it came with a price.

"Because," she said softly, "we had to try. We had to believe we could stop it, even if it was already too late. The fight was never about winning. It was about showing the world that we could still resist. That we could still say no, even as the darkness closed in."

Outside, the first snow of the season began to fall, thick and heavy. It wasn't the gentle, peaceful snow of childhood memories, but a foreboding blanket, a herald of the darkness to come. The clock ticked louder in the silence, each second a countdown to the inevitable.

Emma turned her gaze to the window, her face pale. "It's starting. The last Christmas."

As the first stroke of midnight sounded, the world outside seemed to hold its breath. The snow fell harder, and the stars vanished behind a dark, thickened sky. Santa's power had reached its peak.

There would be no Christmas after this. No new year. No hope. Only the cold, eternal reign of Satan.

And as Emma sat there with her comrades, knowing they had failed, she realized that there was one last gift Santa had to give.

The world was his now, and it always had been.

The Christmas Shroud

Every year, the Johnson family gathered at their ancestral home for Christmas Eve, a tradition that had been passed down through generations. The house was always filled with the warm glow of holiday lights, the sweet scent of pine and cinnamon, and the sound of festive music drifting from the speakers. It was a night for family, for laughter, and for the comfort of knowing that, no matter what happened throughout the year, this one night would always remain the same.

But this year felt different.

Maggie Johnson stood at the kitchen counter, watching her husband, Dan, and their two children, Leah and Jake, as they set the table for dinner. The fire crackled in the hearth, and outside, snow fell in soft, heavy sheets. It was perfect—the kind of perfect that only existed in holiday movies. Yet, there was a strange sense of unease gnawing at Maggie's insides, a feeling she couldn't shake.

"Everything okay, hon?" Dan's voice broke through her thoughts, and she turned to see him standing behind her, holding two glasses of wine.

"I'm fine," she said, though her voice felt hollow, even to her own ears. "It's just... strange. It's always the same, you know? Year after year, we do the same things, have the same dinner, the same speeches... I just feel like something is different this year. Like something is missing."

Dan chuckled lightly, his smile warm and reassuring. "It's just the stress of the holidays, Maggie. You know how you get. Don't overthink it. This is our family's time to come together, to enjoy each other. Nothing more."

But Maggie wasn't so sure. She had felt this way before, a quiet whisper at the back of her mind telling her that there was something darker at play. For years, she had ignored it, buried it under the joy and comfort of the tradition, but tonight, it seemed louder than ever.

As the evening wore on, the family settled around the grand dining table, a feast laid out before them. The food was always abundant—turkey, mashed potatoes, green beans, cranberry sauce—but somehow, tonight, it all felt... off. The mashed potatoes were too creamy, the turkey too rich. Even the wine tasted thick and cloying, as though it were laced with something other than alcohol.

"Is it just me, or does this wine taste a little strange?" Leah asked, her voice a bit more slurred than usual.

Maggie looked up, startled. Leah was only sixteen. She shouldn't be drinking this much wine. But when Maggie glanced at her, she saw the same blank, distant look that had come over her face the past few years, the look she had always assumed was just the effects of a busy holiday season.

"No, it's just the wine," Dan said quickly, waving it off. "Nothing to worry about."

But Maggie couldn't ignore the feeling that gnawed at her. Her skin prickled, her breath came in shallow gasps. Something was wrong. Something had been wrong for years, and now it was reaching its breaking point.

As they moved into the living room after dinner, the same rituals took place. The children opened their gifts, each one more extravagant than the last, though Maggie noticed they all seemed a little... wrong. The toys weren't things her children had asked for, or even wanted. Leah had received a porcelain doll with vacant, soulless eyes, while Jake had opened a box to find an ornate chess set, though he had no interest in the game.

The evening wore on, but the laughter felt hollow. The crackle of the fire grew more oppressive. Maggie couldn't take her eyes off the Christmas tree. It stood at the corner of the room, its lights dimmer than usual, its tinsel tarnished, as if the tree itself were rotting from within.

Suddenly, it hit her. The family wasn't gathering for Christmas. They weren't just celebrating the holiday. This was a ritual. A ritual they had been performing for years, maybe decades, and they had never questioned it.

Maggie stood up abruptly, her chair scraping across the floor, the sound too loud in the room. "I need some air," she said, her voice trembling.

Dan and the kids didn't respond, their eyes glazed over, staring into the fire as if transfixed by it. Maggie stepped outside into the cold, but it didn't help. The snow didn't feel real; the air didn't feel crisp. The world seemed muffled, almost as if it were being viewed through a thick fog. She turned back toward the house, her heart racing, and as she approached the door, she saw something that made her blood run cold.

A figure stood in the window, its outline barely visible in the glow of the candles inside. It was tall, with a dark cloak draped over its frame, but it wasn't the figure itself that terrified her. It was the eyes. The eyes that gleamed with a fire that burned too hot, too red. And they were looking directly at her.

She rushed back inside, slamming the door behind her. But when she entered the living room, her family was gone. The tree was gone. The house itself was different, darker, as if it had become part of the very shadows that loomed outside.

"Maggie," Dan's voice came from behind her, but it was wrong. His voice was deeper now, colder. She turned to find him standing in the doorway, his features twisted in a way that was no longer human. His smile stretched unnaturally wide, revealing teeth too sharp, too jagged.

"Welcome home," he said, his voice echoing in the empty room.

Maggie stumbled back, her breath coming in gasps. The realization hit her like a hammer to the chest. She had known, deep down, that there was something unnatural about their Christmas gatherings. Something dark. But now she saw it clearly—the rituals had never been for Christmas. They had been for something else, something far worse. Every year, they had invited Satan into their home, feeding him with their souls, their joy, their belief.

The presents, the laughter, the feasts—they had all been part of a sacrifice. And now, it was too late. Maggie had already been claimed.

She looked around, her heart sinking as she saw her children, now standing motionless in the corner of the room, their eyes empty and lifeless. They were no longer her children. They were slaves, part of the dark pact that had bound them all.

"Maggie, don't worry," Dan's voice cut through her thoughts. "This is just the beginning. The world will soon be ours. We'll all be together forever, serving him."

As the fire flickered and the last echoes of Christmas carols faded into the night, Maggie felt the coldest of shrouds descend over her. The Christmas she had once known, the joy she had once felt, was gone. In its place was an eternal darkness, a fate sealed by the very traditions she had once cherished.

The last Christmas had come, and with it, the end of everything.

The Curse of Saint Nick

Dr. Nathaniel Blackwood was a scholar of obscure history, the kind of man who spent sleepless nights hunched over ancient texts and forgotten manuscripts, seeking truths that had long been buried. His obsession had led him down many dark paths, but it was the history of Saint Nicholas that had captivated him the most in recent months.

To the modern world, Saint Nicholas was a kindly figure, a jolly old man who brought gifts to children and symbolized the spirit of giving. But to Blackwood, the man behind the myth had always been more complex, his history buried under layers of folklore and tradition. What he had discovered, in his late-night research, was not the benevolent patron saint revered by millions, but a much darker origin.

It had begun innocently enough, a simple search for historical facts surrounding the origins of Christmas. Blackwood had expected to uncover tales of generosity, perhaps a few murmurings of early Christian influences. But what he found went far deeper, to a time long before Saint Nicholas became the symbol of kindness.

The ancient texts he uncovered told of a man who had once been revered in a different context, a man not of compassion but of coercion. Saint Nicholas had once been a figure associated with punishment, a figure who exacted cruel retribution on those who had defied him. His legend spoke of a man who ruled over an army of creatures, not elves, but darker, more sinister beings, whose duty was to ensure that the souls of the wicked would never escape their torment.

The more Blackwood dug, the darker the truths became. He learned that Saint Nicholas was once worshipped by a pagan cult, a man who wore the cloak of a god, a ruler of the underworld who carried out the bidding of forces far beyond human comprehension. The cheerful image of Saint Nick, with his sack of gifts and rosy cheeks, was a mask—a disguise meant to veil a deeper, more insidious truth. He was not a gift-bringer but a harbinger of suffering, a demon clothed in the guise of a saint.

As Blackwood pieced the puzzle together, the boundaries between historical fact and myth began to blur. He found references to rituals performed in honor of Saint Nicholas, rituals that involved sacrifices to ensure prosperity and safety for those who worshipped him. These were not the innocent rituals of a church; they were rites steeped in blood, acts designed to bind the souls of the living to the service of something darker.

His obsession grew. He began to see Saint Nicholas not as a man who had been lost to history, but as something far more dangerous, something alive beneath the layers of centuries. The more he read, the more his mind seemed to unravel. He spent days in his study, his room filled with the musty scent of old papers and the flickering light of candles, as if the darkness of the room was seeping into his very soul.

The break came when Blackwood uncovered an ancient manuscript that had been sealed away for centuries. It was said to contain the original incantations used to summon Saint Nicholas, and the words he read seemed to speak directly to him, as if the old pages were alive with some malevolent force. The writing beckoned him, whispering promises of knowledge and power in exchange for his unwavering devotion.

The night he decided to read the incantations aloud, the atmosphere in his study shifted. The air grew heavy, oppressive, and the shadows in the room seemed to stretch and curl, twisting like serpents around the edges of his vision. His voice trembled as he spoke the ancient words, the syllables foreign on his tongue. It felt as though the room itself was listening, waiting.

At first, nothing happened. The room remained dark and still, but then he heard it. A low chuckle, deep and guttural, reverberating in the corners of his mind. Blackwood's heart raced. He tried to shake off the sensation, but the laughter grew louder, more insistent, until it felt as though the sound were coming from within his very chest.

The figure that appeared before him was not the jovial Santa Claus of Christmas cards. No, this was something far older, far darker. Cloaked in a robe as black as the night itself, his face hidden beneath a shadowy hood, Saint Nicholas stood before him, his eyes burning with an unnatural light. The air around him crackled with an electric charge, and Blackwood could feel his own pulse quickening, as if the very fabric of his existence was beginning to unravel.

"You have awakened me," the figure spoke, his voice low and cold, like the whisper of a thousand winter winds. "You have sought the truth, and now you will serve me."

Blackwood felt the chill of his words seep into his bones. He had done what no man had dared before—he had summoned Saint Nicholas, but not as the saint of generosity and goodwill. No, he had called forth the true Saint Nicholas, the dark spirit who ruled over the damned, the one who would claim the souls of the wicked for eternity.

Fear gripped Blackwood, but it was too late. The darkness enveloped him, consuming him whole. His mind, once sharp and clear, began to dissolve, the edges blurring as the presence of the ancient being filled every corner of his consciousness.

"Why?" Blackwood managed to whisper, his voice trembling with terror.

"You sought the truth," the figure replied, its voice now all-encompassing. "And the truth is this—there is no salvation, no redemption. There is only power. You have been chosen, as I was chosen, as all who walk this path are chosen. Your soul belongs to me now, as does the soul of every man who dares to seek the truth behind the veil."

Blackwood tried to resist, but his will was no match for the overwhelming presence of the spirit. He felt himself sinking into a void, his thoughts no longer his own. The scholar who had once prided himself on his knowledge and intellect was now a vessel, a conduit for something far darker than he had ever imagined.

As the darkness swallowed him whole, the last thought that flickered through his mind was the realization that the true curse of Saint Nicholas was not his origin, nor his power—it was the insidious, irresistible pull of the truth itself. Those who sought to uncover the secrets of the world were doomed, not to enlightenment, but to damnation.

In that moment, Blackwood understood. Some truths were never meant to be found.

And with that, Saint Nicholas claimed another soul.

The Wreath of Doom

Every year, without fail, the Franklin family hung their Christmas wreath on the door. It had been a tradition passed down through generations, a simple ritual that marked the start of the holiday season. The wreath was nothing special, a simple circle of pine branches adorned with red ribbons and small ornaments, but to the Franklins, it was a symbol of home, warmth, and the joy of the season. Little did they know, it was a harbinger of something far darker.

It started small. One winter night, shortly after they had hung the wreath, strange things began to happen. It began with odd noises—soft scratching sounds on the door that no one could explain. At first, it seemed harmless, just the wind or the house settling. But as the days wore on, the sounds grew louder, more persistent. Each time they heard the scratching, the family would go to the door, only to find nothing. No animal tracks. No sign of anything out of the ordinary.

Then came the dreams. At first, they were disjointed—strange visions of shadows moving outside their windows, whispers in the dark. But over time, the dreams became more vivid, more real. Each family member began to dream of a man—a tall, dark figure cloaked in black, his face hidden beneath a hood. He would stand at the door, staring at them with eyes that glowed like embers. Each time they awoke, the man would be gone, but they felt his presence linger, suffocating and cold.

It was Eleanor, the matriarch of the family, who first realized something was wrong. She had been the one to hang the wreath that year, as she had done every year before. But this year, there was something different about it. The moment she touched it, a chill ran up her spine. The wreath, with its festive red ribbons and green pine needles, seemed to pulse with a life of its own. She thought it was just her imagination, a fleeting moment of unease, but when she looked closer, she saw that the ornaments on the wreath were not as they appeared. They were twisted, dark, almost malevolent, and they seemed to move ever so slightly when she wasn't looking directly at them.

Eleanor tried to shake the feeling, but she couldn't. That night, as she prepared dinner, she noticed a faint smell in the air—a rotten, fetid stench that seemed to come from nowhere. She opened the windows, trying to air out the house, but the smell remained. It lingered, filling the rooms and seeping into her very bones.

The following evening, as Christmas Eve approached, the situation grew worse. The strange noises continued, and now, the lights in the house flickered intermittently. One by one, the family members began to feel an overwhelming sense of dread, a heaviness that settled over them like a suffocating weight. Their joy for the season slowly faded, replaced by an overwhelming fear that they couldn't explain.

That night, as they gathered for their Christmas dinner, the tension was palpable. The usual cheer of the season was gone, replaced by silence and unease. Each family member sat at the table, their eyes darting nervously around the room. The wreath, still hanging on the door, seemed to loom over them like a silent observer, its dark energy creeping into their thoughts.

Suddenly, the doorbell rang. A chill ran through the room. The family exchanged uneasy glances. It was late—too late for visitors. Eleanor stood, her hand trembling as she reached for the door. She opened it, and there, standing in the cold night, was the man from her dreams. The tall figure, cloaked in black, his face obscured by shadows. His eyes glowed like red embers, burning through the darkness.

"Who are you?" Eleanor asked, her voice barely a whisper.

The figure didn't answer. Instead, he stepped forward, his presence suffocating. As he crossed the threshold, the air grew colder, the shadows in the room seeming to deepen. The family recoiled in fear, but they couldn't move. It was as if they were paralyzed, trapped in the grip of something far stronger than them.

The man raised his hand, and suddenly, the wreath on the door seemed to come to life. It writhed and twisted, the pine branches stretching and snapping like dark tendrils. The ornaments on the wreath burst into flame, but the flames were not bright—they were black, swirling with an otherworldly smoke. The smell of decay grew stronger, and the man's voice, a low, guttural whisper, filled the room.

"You invited me in," he said. His voice was like gravel being ground together, low and menacing. "You hang the wreath every year, believing it's just a tradition. But you've never understood what it truly is. It is a mark, a brand, a gift given by the one who waits in the dark."

Eleanor tried to speak, to shout, but her voice was trapped in her throat. The man moved closer, his presence suffocating, his eyes burning with an unnatural light. The wreath continued to twist and writhe, now fully alive, its dark tendrils creeping across the floor like serpents, reaching toward the family.

"You are mine," the man said, his voice now a growl. "Every year, you invite me in. And every year, I take something from you."

The room seemed to close in on them, the walls narrowing, the air thickening. The family struggled, but they couldn't break free. The wreath was a curse, an ancient pact made long ago, a pact that had bound their family to Satan's will. Each year, the wreath claimed a piece of their soul, and now, on this Christmas Eve, the final price was due.

One by one, the family members fell to the ground, their bodies twitching, their minds consumed by terror. The man raised his hands, and with a final whisper, the wreath seemed to erupt in a blinding flash of black light.

When the light faded, the house was silent. The wreath was gone, and so were the Franklins. In their place, the tall figure stood, his form now fully revealed. His face, if it could be called a face, was a grotesque mask of twisted, leering smiles, and his eyes glowed brighter than ever. The man turned and walked toward the door, his footsteps echoing like a death knell.

The wreath, now gone from the door, had claimed its final prize. The Franklins were no more, their souls absorbed into the darkness.

And as the man disappeared into the cold night, the wind whispered the same words he had spoken before:

"Every year, you invited me in. Every year, I took what was mine."

The Night Before Doom

Maggie lay in her bed, staring at the ceiling, wide-eyed and restless. The clock on her nightstand read 11:48 PM, and the usual Christmas Eve excitement felt hollow tonight, like a distant memory. The tree in the corner of her room was adorned with twinkling lights and a star on top, but it was the shadowed corners of her room that seemed to draw her attention. She had always loved Christmas, the magic in the air, the promise of gifts and joy. But tonight, something was different.

Her parents had gone to bed early, leaving her alone in the quiet of the house. She could hear the faint sounds of wind howling outside, and the creak of the house settling. But it wasn't the weather that kept her awake—it was the dream she'd had.

She had dreamt of Santa. But it wasn't the jolly man in the red suit that she had been taught to expect. No, in the dream, Santa was something much darker, more sinister. He sat atop a throne made of charred bones, his eyes glowing a fiery red as he surveyed the world beneath him. Around him, the world was burning. Trees were ablaze, homes reduced to ashes, and the sky was filled with dark, swirling clouds. It was a world in torment, a world in agony, and at the center of it all sat Santa, his grin twisted and cruel.

Maggie had woken in a cold sweat, her heart racing. The dream had been so vivid, so real, that it felt like more than just a nightmare. She had tried to shake it off, but it clung to her, gnawing at her insides. What was it? A warning? A premonition? She didn't know, but she couldn't get rid of the feeling that something terrible was about to happen.

As the minutes ticked by, the house seemed to grow colder. Maggie pulled her blanket tighter around her shoulders, trying to ignore the strange feeling creeping up her spine. The wind outside howled louder now, its eerie whistle filling the night air. It sounded almost like a voice—low and guttural, like a whispering chant. She tried to block it out, to tell herself it was just the wind, but the more she listened, the clearer it became.

Suddenly, a thud echoed from downstairs, followed by the faint sound of shuffling footsteps. Maggie's heart skipped a beat. It was late—far too late for anyone to be awake. She hesitated, unsure whether to get out of bed or to hide beneath the covers. But the curiosity tugged at her, urging her to move. She quietly slipped out of bed and tiptoed to the door, opening it just a crack to peer down the hallway.

At first, she saw nothing. The house was dark, and the shadows seemed to stretch unnaturally. But then, from the corner of her eye, she noticed something. A figure, tall and cloaked, moved silently through the living room. The figure wore a dark robe, and its face was obscured by a hood, but the red glow of its eyes pierced through the darkness like burning embers.

Maggie's breath caught in her throat. It couldn't be him. She had to be imagining it. But as she watched, the figure moved toward the tree. It knelt in front of the fireplace, its hands reaching for the stockings hanging there. There was no mistaking it now. This was no ordinary visitor.

Santa.

But not the Santa she knew from the stories. This Santa was dark, terrifying, and far more powerful than she had ever imagined. Maggie backed away from the door, her heart hammering in her chest. She felt rooted to the spot, unable to tear her eyes away from the creature moving silently below.

The figure turned, and Maggie could swear she saw a smile on his face. A smile that was more like a leer, full of malice. The air around her seemed to grow colder, and the flickering light from the tree cast twisted shadows across the walls. The figure stood up, the sound of his cloak brushing the floor like a whisper of death. He moved closer to the staircase.

Maggie's legs felt like lead as she stumbled backward into her room. She slammed the door behind her and locked it, her hands trembling. She didn't know what to do, what to think. She was certain now—the dream, the figure downstairs, they were connected. But how? And why? What was happening?

The wind outside had grown into a full-blown storm, and the sounds of chanting had intensified, louder now, as though they were coming from inside the walls. Maggie squeezed her eyes shut, trying to block it out. But then, as if on cue, she heard it. A soft knock at her door.

At first, she thought it was just her imagination. But then, it came again, louder this time. Three knocks, slow and deliberate.

"Maggie," a voice whispered from the other side, a voice that was both familiar and terrifying. "Maggie, it's time."

Her heart skipped a beat as the door slowly creaked open. Maggie couldn't move. She couldn't speak. The figure from downstairs stood in the doorway, the dim light from the hallway casting long, twisted shadows on the floor. His eyes glowed brighter now, and the smile on his face was impossibly wide.

"Maggie," the figure said again, his voice a low, echoing growl. "You've been chosen. You're part of the gift now. A child of the dark."

Terror surged through her body, but before she could scream, the figure stepped forward, his hand cold as ice. He touched her shoulder, and in that instant, she felt her body go numb, as though her very soul was being ripped from her.

"Don't be afraid," the voice whispered. "You're not the first. And you won't be the last."

As the figure dragged her toward the door, Maggie's mind raced. The dream. The burning world. The man on the throne. She had seen it all before, and now, she understood. The world was ending, and tonight, Christmas Eve, was the night it all began. Santa was no longer a symbol of joy and cheer. He was the herald of doom, the servant of something far darker. And she had been chosen to join his army.

But as the figure led her outside into the raging storm, Maggie realized with a sinking heart that it wasn't just her. It wasn't just this Christmas. The end had begun for everyone, and no one would be spared.

The world would burn. And there was nothing anyone could do to stop it.

Maggie's screams were lost in the wind as the storm raged on.

Satan's Toymaker

Elias Garvey had always been a man of simple pleasures. He was a toymaker by trade, and for years, he found satisfaction in crafting little wooden soldiers, dollhouses, and train sets. His hands were rough with calluses, but his heart swelled with pride each time a child's face lit up with joy upon receiving one of his creations. To Elias, there was nothing more beautiful than the innocent happiness a child could find in something he had made with his own hands.

But lately, things had begun to change. It started with a request from a well-dressed man who appeared one brisk November morning at Elias's door. The man introduced himself as Mr. Crowley, a wealthy businessman from the city. He had heard about Elias's work and was interested in commissioning a new kind of toy—something more than the simple wooden toys Elias was known for.

"Something magical," Mr. Crowley had said, his dark eyes glinting in the dim light. "A toy that would capture the true essence of Christmas. Something that would stir a child's heart in ways they've never known before."

Elias had been intrigued by the idea, though it felt oddly unsettling. He was no stranger to magic, not in the sense that others might be. He had a certain understanding of the craft, inherited from his father, who had been a toymaker as well. But his father's toys had been harmless, innocent. The ones Mr. Crowley was asking for, though, seemed to have a weight to them—a kind of darkness that Elias could feel even as the words left the man's lips.

"I can give you the materials, Elias," Mr. Crowley continued, handing over a small leather pouch. "But you must do this yourself. You're the only one with the skill to bring these toys to life."

Inside the pouch, Elias found a strange mixture of herbs, oils, and small bone fragments, each more unnatural than the last. There was also a small, tattered book, its pages yellowed and worn, inscribed with symbols that seemed to burn when he looked at them. He recognized them as ancient, arcane markings—runes from an older time, older than he cared to admit.

Despite his hesitation, Elias had agreed to the commission. It wasn't for the money—no, Elias didn't need wealth. But something in the depths of his mind stirred as he looked at the items Mr. Crowley had left him. He began to think of the children who would receive these toys—how their joy might surpass anything he had ever seen before. Perhaps, he reasoned, this was the key to creating something truly extraordinary.

For weeks, Elias worked tirelessly, his fingers trembling as he shaped the toys. They began to take form—small wooden dolls, each intricately carved, with eyes that gleamed in the flickering candlelight of his workshop. He used the oils and herbs to coat the wooden bodies, the scent thick and musky, like incense, as he whispered the incantations written in the old book.

As the final touches were added, Elias couldn't shake the feeling that something was wrong. The toys felt... alive, somehow. They seemed to watch him, their eyes following his every move. He dismissed the thought as paranoia—after all, he was a toymaker, not a magician. Yet, every night as he closed his workshop door, he could hear faint giggles—high-pitched and childlike—emanating from inside.

On Christmas Eve, the first batch of toys was delivered. The parents who received them were overjoyed. They marveled at the craftsmanship, the detail, the realism of the toys, and the children who received them were enchanted. Elias watched as one by one, the children opened their gifts, their faces lighting up with an intensity he had never seen before.

But then things began to change. At first, it was subtle. The children became unusually quiet, their eyes distant. They played with their new toys in a trance-like state, murmuring to them in a language Elias couldn't understand. The parents laughed it off, thinking it was just the excitement of Christmas, but Elias felt a deep unease gnawing at his stomach.

The next morning, when the sun rose, the children were no longer themselves. They had changed. Their once innocent faces were twisted in ways that couldn't be explained—pale, their eyes now black as coal, void of life. They no longer spoke or played. Instead, they stared ahead, unmoving, as though waiting for something.

Elias tried to visit the families, but each time, the door was slammed in his face. When he managed to sneak a glance through the windows, he saw the children inside—standing perfectly still, their toys beside them, their eyes locked onto something invisible. Something dark.

Desperate, Elias returned to his workshop and examined the toys. He had to know what had gone wrong. As he turned one of the dolls over in his hands, he saw it—the faintest of markings etched beneath the wood, almost invisible, yet unmistakably there. A symbol. The same symbol that had appeared in the ancient book Mr. Crowley had given him. The runes had not been meant to animate the toys in the way he had thought. No, they were meant for something far darker.

The toys weren't meant to bring joy. They were meant to take control. The children were no longer their own. They were being consumed, transformed—slowly turning into servants of something far more sinister than any of them could have imagined. Elias had unwittingly bound their souls to Satan himself.

Panicked, Elias tried to destroy the toys. He burned them, smashed them, cast them into the deepest lake near his shop. But each time, they returned—creeping back into the homes of the children, always finding their way back to where they belonged. The toys could not be destroyed.

The curse was too strong.

Elias became obsessed. He searched the book, but the more he read, the more he understood. The toys were never meant to be destroyed—they were instruments, anchors, tools for a far greater purpose. The toys were the vessels through which Satan's power would spread—through the children, through their families. It was the beginning of an invasion. The beginning of a kingdom being built, one soul at a time.

One night, as he sat in his workshop, surrounded by the toys he had created, Elias realized something terrible. The toys had always known what they were meant to do. And so, too, did he.

The door to his shop opened, and there, standing in the doorway, was Mr. Crowley. His dark eyes gleamed with satisfaction.

"You've done well, Elias," Mr. Crowley said, his voice smooth and cold. "The children are mine now. The world will be ours."

Elias could do nothing but stare at the man, realizing with horror that he had never been the maker. He had always been the made.

The toys were never meant to be destroyed. They were never meant to bring joy. They were meant to create an army—an army of darkness—and Elias had unknowingly been its first soldier.

And now, there was no way out.

The Fallen Saint

Father Dominic had always been a man of unwavering faith, a servant of the Church for over thirty years. His life had been simple, marked by routine and dedication to his parishioners. He spent his days in prayer, his nights in vigil, and though there were moments of doubt, he always found comfort in the sanctity of his calling. But tonight was different.

He sat in the small, dimly lit confessional, waiting for the soul who would come to him for absolution. It was Christmas Eve, a time when people gathered to seek forgiveness, to repent for their sins, to prepare their hearts for the coming of Christ. But this year, there was something oppressive in the air—a weight that seemed to hang over the Church, something he couldn't shake. It was as though the very walls of the building were holding their breath.

The door creaked open, and a figure entered the confessional. Father Dominic barely glanced up, expecting the usual confession, the mundane admissions of guilt over minor transgressions. But the voice that greeted him was not the soft, familiar tone of a parishioner seeking penance.

"I've come to tell you a story, Father," the voice said, deep and gravelly, filled with an ancient sorrow. It sent a chill through Father Dominic's spine. The words felt wrong—too heavy, too deliberate.

Father Dominic instinctively reached for the rosary hanging from his waist, his knuckles white from the pressure. He could feel the presence in the room, and it was like nothing he had ever encountered before. It was an overwhelming darkness, seeping into the cracks of his soul.

"A story?" Father Dominic replied, his voice steady, though his heart raced. "Who are you?"

There was a pause, and then a low laugh that seemed to vibrate the walls around them. The figure in the confessional shifted, leaning closer, and the scent of burning incense mixed with something far darker—decay, sulfur.

"I once was an angel," the voice continued, its tone both seductive and sinister. "I was one of the highest, entrusted with the most sacred of duties. But pride... pride is a terrible thing, Father. And I fell. Do you know what it feels like to fall from Heaven?"

Father Dominic's blood ran cold. He gripped the edge of the confessional, his knuckles trembling.

"You... you are not who you say you are," he whispered, a tremor in his voice. "This is blasphemy. Leave now, before I call for help."

The figure laughed again, but this time, it was different. It was a laugh that echoed through the very core of Father Dominic's being. He could hear the voice shifting, morphing into something more ancient, more dreadful.

"You don't believe me, Father? You don't believe that the one you call Saint Nicholas—the one who brings joy and gifts on Christmas—is a fallen angel? Do you not see it? The lies you've been fed since you were a child. That jolly old man in red, the one who slides down chimneys, the one who comes to children with gifts and cheer—he is not what you think he is. His name is not Santa Claus. His name is Azazel. And he is not here to spread joy."

Father Dominic recoiled, his mind struggling to comprehend the words. He had heard stories, of course—the rumors, the whispers about the origins of Christmas. But never had he imagined it to be true. Never had he dared to believe that the spirit of Christmas was not a force for good, but for something far darker.

"Azazel?" Father Dominic croaked, his voice barely audible. "No... no, that's impossible. Santa—Saint Nicholas—he's a symbol of kindness, of charity."

A rasping breath filled the confessional, thick with the weight of ages. The figure's voice now sounded like a thousand souls crying out in torment.

"Saint Nicholas was once an angel, Father. A guardian of the innocent, a protector of the pure. But his pride, his desire to be adored, led him to fall. He was cast from Heaven, and in his fall, he took on the mantle of something darker. He is no saint. He is the Devil's servant. His mission, his true purpose, is not to bring joy—but to take souls."

Father Dominic's heart pounded in his chest, his hands gripping the arms of the confessional as though they were the only thing keeping him anchored to reality.

"You lie," he spat. "You are an imposter, a demon trying to deceive me. I will not listen to your lies."

But the voice didn't waver. It only grew more insistent, more terrifying.

"Look into your heart, Father," the voice urged, growing darker still. "Look into the very soul of the holiday you worship. Christmas... it was never meant to be a time of peace. It was always a time of reckoning. The gifts, the laughter, the cheer—these are nothing but tools. Tools to gather the souls of the faithful. To lull them into a false sense of security, to have them worship the very thing that will drag them to Hell."

Father Dominic gasped. The air around him thickened, suffocating him. His vision blurred, and the sound of the confessional door creaking open echoed in his ears. He tried to speak, but his voice caught in his throat.

"You see, Father, you have been blessed with the sight," the voice continued, its tone softening, almost affectionate. "That's why I've come to you. I need your soul—your purity. For you, too, are part of my plan. You have served the light for too long. It is time for you to join me in the dark."

Father Dominic's eyes widened as he felt something—cold, malevolent—brush against his mind, invading his thoughts, pushing against his will. He could feel the presence of the figure in the confessional now, looming over him, suffocating him with its power.

"No... I won't join you," Father Dominic managed to gasp, struggling to keep his grip on the cross hanging around his neck. "I will fight you. I will expose you for what you are."

The figure laughed again, a sound that made Father Dominic's blood run cold.

"You already have, Father. You already have. You see, Christmas is not just a holiday. It is the time when souls are ripe for the taking. And you... you, my dear priest, are the final sacrifice. You've been chosen."

Before Father Dominic could react, the figure surged forward, and with a swift motion, the darkness enveloped him. His body trembled as the weight of the presence crushed him, his mind spiraling into darkness.

The confessional door creaked open, and the figure stepped out. He stood tall, his form now fully revealed in the flickering candlelight—a twisted, corrupted version of Saint Nicholas, his red suit torn and stained with darkness, his eyes glowing with a malevolent fire.

"I told you, Father," the figure whispered, bending low to whisper in his ear. "I am not Santa Claus. I am the Fallen Saint. And tonight, you are mine."

Father Dominic screamed, but it was already too late. The darkness had already consumed him, and with it, his soul was bound for eternity.

Outside, the snow continued to fall gently, blanketing the earth in white. Christmas had arrived. But for Father Dominic, it was the beginning of an endless night.

The Christmas Massacre

The snow was thick that night, blanketing the world in an eerie, suffocating silence. The Johnson family had been living in their remote cabin for years, away from the noise of the world, away from the bustle of society, and most importantly, away from Christmas. For them, the holiday had always been a time of darkness, a reminder of loss, of painful memories that had never faded. They tried to ignore it, but even out here, in the deep woods, there was no escaping the season. It crept in through the cracks, tugging at their hearts, whispering in the wind.

That Christmas Eve, the house felt more isolated than ever. Inside, the fire crackled in the hearth, casting long shadows on the walls. Emily, the mother, sat by the window, her face pressed against the glass as she looked out into the night. Her husband, Mark, sat with the children, trying to make the evening feel festive, but it was clear to all of them that it wasn't. No amount of decorations, no forced cheer could mask the sadness that clung to them.

Then came the knock.

At first, Emily thought it was just the wind, the ice shifting against the wood. But then came the second knock, louder this time, more deliberate. Mark stood up and walked toward the door. A chill swept through the house, a sudden drop in temperature that made the hairs on Emily's neck rise. She glanced nervously at the children, who had all stopped talking, sensing something was wrong. The silence felt unnatural.

Mark opened the door, his breath visible in the air as he stepped outside.

The man standing there was tall, impossibly so, his figure obscured by the swirling snow. He wore a thick red coat, stained dark with what could have been dirt or blood, and his boots were heavy, caked in snow and mud. His face was obscured by a long, thick beard, but his eyes—those eyes—were glowing, a deep, unnatural red, like embers smoldering in the darkness.

"Can I help you?" Mark asked, his voice betraying the unease creeping up his spine.

The man's lips curled into a smile that was too wide, too deep, a grin that stretched unnaturally across his face. "Ho ho ho," he chuckled, but it was not a jovial sound. It was guttural, mocking, and full of something far darker.

Mark stepped back, unsure if he should slam the door shut or invite the stranger in. The man outside gave him no choice. Before Mark could react, the figure pushed the door open with ease, stepping into the dimly lit cabin as though he owned the place.

"Welcome to your final Christmas," the man said, his voice low and steady, like a whisper in the wind.

Emily's heart began to race. She tried to speak, but no words came out. Mark stood frozen, his mouth agape, unable to comprehend what was happening. The stranger's presence filled the room, heavy and oppressive. The children, huddled in the corner, stared at the man with wide eyes, sensing something far more sinister than their parents did.

"I've been watching you," the man continued, his voice becoming more melodic, almost soothing. "All of you. I've been waiting for this moment."

"Who... who are you?" Mark stammered.

The man's grin widened. "Who am I? I am the spirit of Christmas, of course. The one who comes to reward the good and punish the wicked."

But his words didn't ring true. Emily could feel the coldness of his presence, something far older, more malicious than anything she had ever experienced. This wasn't Santa. This wasn't a jolly man bringing gifts. This was something else entirely.

The figure reached into his coat and pulled out a sack. It was large, far larger than it should have been for a man of his size, and it bulged unnaturally, as though it contained something far more than toys. As he opened the sack, Emily's blood ran cold. Inside were bodies—dead, frozen bodies of children, their eyes wide open in horror, their mouths frozen in screams. Their faces were pale, blue with frostbite, their limbs twisted in unnatural positions. The sack was a macabre collection of lifelessness, each child an offering.

"You... you killed them?" Emily whispered, horrified.

The man's eyes gleamed. "Not killed, no. They are not dead. They are simply... claimed. They belong to me now, just as you will."

Emily stumbled back, her breath shallow, her vision blurring as the room began to spin. Mark's hand gripped her arm, his face pale as the reality of the situation set in.

"You see," the man continued, his voice now dripping with dark amusement, "every year I bring gifts to the good, to the ones who believe. But this year, it's different. This year, I'm taking something far more valuable than belief. This year, I take your souls."

The words hit like a sledgehammer. Emily's knees buckled, but she caught herself against the wall. "No... no, please," she begged, her voice breaking. "What do you want from us?"

The man's red eyes bored into hers. "I want nothing from you. You are already mine. The moment you accepted the lie of Christmas, the moment you celebrated this time of year, you bound yourselves to me. You became part of the ritual. You, too, will be added to the collection."

Mark backed away, trying to shield the children, but it was futile. The man stepped forward, his presence swallowing up the warmth of the room. He reached out, his cold fingers brushing Mark's shoulder, and instantly, Mark's body went stiff. He fell to the floor, eyes glazed over, lifeless.

Emily screamed, pulling the children back, but it was too late. The man walked toward her, his steps slow and deliberate. She tried to move, to run, but her body wouldn't obey. Fear froze her in place.

"You see, Emily," the man said, his voice now almost tender, "this is the end. The end of mankind's hope. I've watched you all for centuries, waiting for the right moment. Christmas was never meant to be a time of joy. It was meant to be a time of reckoning. A time for me to gather those who have given in to the darkness."

The man's eyes glowed brighter, and suddenly, the room was filled with the sound of distant, unholy laughter. The walls seemed to pulse, the very air vibrating with an unnatural energy.

Emily looked at her children, their faces filled with terror, their small bodies trembling. She realized, in that final, terrible moment, that there was no escape. There had never been. The Christmas spirit she had tried so hard to protect was not one of love, but of control—a lie woven into the very fabric of society. And she had fallen for it.

The man—the thing that had once been Santa—reached out to her, and with a single touch, the world went dark.

Outside, the snow continued to fall, untouched by time, as if nothing had ever happened at all. And in the silence, the last remnants of humanity were snuffed out, consumed by the darkness of Christmas.

In the end, there was no joy, no cheer. Only the cold grip of death.

The Chimney of Souls

The Johnson family had always been close-knit. Every Christmas Eve, they gathered around the fireplace in their home, lighting the fire, hanging stockings, and preparing for the annual tradition of waiting for Santa. It was a warm, comforting ritual, one that had been passed down through the generations. This year, however, was different. There was an unspoken tension in the air, a heaviness that none of them could shake. The air felt colder, despite the fire crackling in the hearth. And as the wind howled outside, the family sat together, unaware of the darkness that was slowly creeping into their home.

It began with a strange noise in the chimney. At first, it was just a faint scratching, like something—or someone—was trying to make its way down. The noise grew louder as the night wore on, more insistent, like the claws of a beast scraping against stone. At first, Mr. Johnson, trying to keep the peace, laughed it off. "Just a squirrel or something," he said. "Nothing to worry about." But his words felt hollow, as if even he didn't believe them.

As midnight approached, the family gathered around the fireplace, waiting for the inevitable thud of Santa's entry. The children, Tommy and Sarah, were eagerly anticipating the gifts they'd find under the tree in the morning. Mrs. Johnson, though, couldn't shake the unease that had settled in her stomach. She had always loved Christmas, but tonight, it felt wrong—unnatural. The air was too still. The silence, too deep. The fire seemed to flicker strangely, casting long shadows that danced on the walls like twisted figures.

Suddenly, the scraping noise from the chimney grew louder, sharper. It was as though something was clawing its way down, something far heavier than a mere Santa Claus would be. The children jumped at the sound, their eyes wide with confusion and a growing sense of fear. "Mom, Dad, what's that sound?" Sarah whispered, her voice trembling.

Before anyone could respond, a low, guttural laugh echoed through the chimney, one that wasn't like the jolly chuckles they had all grown up hearing in the stories. This laugh was dark, hollow, as if it came from deep within the earth itself. It rattled their bones, making their blood run cold.

"That's not Santa," Mr. Johnson muttered under his breath, his face pale. He stood up, looking around as though searching for something to explain the noise. But there was nothing.

And then, just as the clock struck midnight, the chimney erupted with a violent crash, and a figure descended into the living room. He was tall, impossibly so, his dark red coat torn at the seams, his face obscured by a long, black beard. His eyes glowed an eerie, fiery orange, and the smell of sulfur filled the room. He didn't land with the soft thud of a man accustomed to sneaking down chimneys—he landed with a sickening thump, as though his body was far heavier than it should have been. His laughter, low and guttural, echoed through the room as he rose to his feet.

The family stood frozen, unable to speak, as the figure turned his gaze toward them. His smile stretched wide, unnatural, his lips curling up in a way that felt wrong, as though they were never meant to be that way.

"Well, well, well," the figure said, his voice thick with malice. "What do we have here? A cozy little family, waiting for the 'jolly old man' to deliver their gifts."

Mrs. Johnson felt a cold sweat break out across her forehead. "Who... who are you?" she managed to stammer, her voice quivering. "What do you want?"

The figure's smile grew wider. "I am the one who delivers gifts," he replied slowly, each word dripping with venom. "But not in the way you think. I deliver gifts of a much darker nature."

The family backed away, but the figure seemed to glide forward, his eyes never leaving them. "You see, every year I visit homes like yours. I enter through the chimneys, through the hearths, through the very souls of those who believe. But the truth you've been taught is a lie. I am not here to bring joy. I am here to collect."

The room seemed to close in on them, the fire flickering wildly, the shadows on the walls now shifting, moving with a life of their own. Mrs. Johnson's heart raced, the reality of the situation dawning on her. This wasn't some innocent man in a red suit. This was something much darker, something ancient.

"What do you want from us?" Mr. Johnson asked, his voice hoarse, his throat dry.

The figure chuckled darkly, stepping closer. "Your souls," he said, his voice a whisper that slithered through their minds. "I come to collect them, one family at a time. You've given in to the lie of Christmas. You've welcomed me into your home, opened your hearts to the falsehood of joy and giving. But Christmas is not about love, or peace, or charity. It is about sacrifice. Every chimney I descend into, every hearth I enter, is a ritual. A ritual that binds the souls of those who welcome me. And you, my dear family, are no different."

The family froze. No one moved. The air was thick, heavy with dread. It felt as though the very walls of the house were alive, closing in on them. They couldn't breathe, couldn't think.

"But there is more," the figure continued, his voice now low and coaxing, as though he were trying to lull them into submission. "You see, the moment you accepted Christmas, the moment you invited me in with your belief, you invited darkness into your lives. The gifts, the lights, the feasts—none of it was ever meant for joy. It was always meant for control. Every year, every home I visit, the souls are claimed. One by one, until the last of the believers are mine."

The family, now gripped by terror, realized the truth. Their traditions, their innocent holiday customs, had been part of a ritual that had enslaved them, that had bound their souls to something far darker than they had ever imagined. They were nothing more than pawns in a much greater game, one that had been played for centuries.

As the figure extended his hand toward them, Tommy, the youngest, stepped forward, his face pale and wide-eyed. "Please... no... we didn't mean to..."

The figure's laughter filled the room, echoing off the walls. "Oh, but you did mean to," he said, his voice now a twisted mockery of kindness. "You always have."

With a single motion, the figure reached out and touched Tommy's forehead. The child's body stiffened, and his eyes glazed over. Then, without warning, he collapsed to the floor, lifeless.

Mrs. Johnson screamed, but it was too late. One by one, the figure claimed the souls of the family, their bodies falling motionless as they were dragged into the darkness. The fire in the hearth burned out, leaving nothing but cold ashes.

Outside, the snow continued to fall, soft and silent, blanketing the earth in a cold, lifeless blanket. And in that house, the ritual was complete.

The chimney was now empty, the trap set for the next family who would unknowingly open their doors to the false spirit of Christmas. The man in red was already on his way to the next home, ready to collect what was owed.

For there is no escape from the Chimney of Souls.

The Santanagram

Martin Holloway wasn't the type of man to believe in conspiracy theories. A professor of history at the University of Chicago, he had always prided himself on his analytical mind. His career had been built on facts, evidence, and critical thinking. But all of that changed the day he stumbled upon the Santanagram.

It began innocuously enough. Martin was scrolling through old manuscripts in the university's library archives, researching the roots of Christmas traditions for a lecture he was preparing. He had spent weeks delving into ancient rituals, myths, and the evolution of Saint Nicholas. But it was in the forgotten corners of the library, hidden behind stacks of dusty books, that he found a worn, leather-bound tome that piqued his curiosity.

The book was labeled "The Secret History of Santa Claus," its spine cracked from years of neglect. There were no other markings, no indication of its author, and no publisher. Just the book itself, as if it had been placed there intentionally, waiting for him.

He began reading that night, his mind sharp with intrigue. The text described a far darker history of Santa Claus than Martin had ever imagined. Santa, it claimed, was not a benevolent figure who brought gifts to children; he was a demon—an ancient force who had long manipulated the world through a carefully constructed myth. The book hinted at a conspiracy that stretched back centuries, involving the world's most powerful figures, all of whom were allegedly in league with this dark figure, ensuring his influence persisted through generations.

But it wasn't until the next morning that Martin discovered the key piece of the puzzle. As he leafed through the pages, one cryptic paragraph caught his eye. It described the way Santa had hidden his true name in plain sight, as a joke, perhaps, to mock humanity's ignorance. "Santa's name," the book wrote, "is no more than an anagram for what he truly is: Satan."

S-A-N-T-A.

Martin read it again, his heart beginning to pound in his chest. He laughed nervously, as if the idea was too absurd to entertain. Santa. Satan. It seemed too ridiculous, too simplistic to be anything but a coincidence. But the more he thought about it, the more it gnawed at him. He began to wonder if the entire tradition of Christmas, this beloved celebration of goodwill, had been co-opted by dark forces. He felt the pull of a deeper truth that was hidden beneath centuries of holiday cheer.

For days, he immersed himself in research, connecting dots between the ancient rituals of Yuletide and more sinister pagan rites, tracing the development of Santa Claus through European folklore. He found unsettling connections between modern Christmas celebrations and occult symbolism, from the red robes of Saint Nicholas to the green and red colors of the holiday. Every aspect seemed to reinforce the theory, but it was the global reach of Christmas—its omnipresence—that truly chilled him. How could such a story, so ingrained in the collective consciousness, be anything but part of a larger, more deliberate scheme?

And then, one night, as he sat in his office staring at the stacks of notes he had compiled, a thought hit him with terrifying clarity: the world's leaders were in on it. They weren't simply complicit in the perpetuation of Santa Claus. They were actively supporting the figure, allowing it to control humanity from behind the scenes.

The connections were too precise to ignore. The same global leaders who perpetuated Christmas as a universal holiday were also the ones pushing a neoliberal agenda that undermined individual freedom and empowered corporations. The very institutions of power were aligned with Santa—an ancient force who had masqueraded as a benevolent gift-bringer, while manipulating human desire, greed, and fear. How could it be a coincidence?

Martin's research grew increasingly obsessive. He began to look for patterns in public speeches, in political alliances, in global economic decisions. He found references to "the spirit of giving" used by politicians in speeches, which he had always dismissed as harmless platitudes. But now, he saw them in a new light—symbols, code words, used to reinforce the power structure that Santa, or Satan, had carefully crafted over the centuries.

He could feel his sanity starting to unravel. At night, he began to hear whispers in his apartment, strange murmurs that seemed to emanate from the shadows. He saw Santa's face everywhere: in advertisements, in children's cartoons, in the faces of politicians, in the hands of business magnates. He even thought he saw the same dark eyes, the same twisted smile on the faces of people he passed on the street. There was no escaping it, no place where he could turn and not see the hand of Santa at work.

Desperation set in. Martin contacted old colleagues, trying to warn them, to share what he had uncovered, but they laughed it off, chalking it up to his obsession with conspiracy theories. He was branded a paranoid lunatic. But the more isolated he became, the more certain he was that he was right. There was no going back. He had uncovered something that no one else had seen. The world was under the control of something ancient, something insidious, and it was hidden behind the very traditions that the world celebrated.

It wasn't until one late evening, as Martin sat staring at the television, that he saw it—a broadcast showing world leaders gathered for a holiday charity event, their faces all radiant with faux joy. There, in the middle of the group, standing above all the others, was a man dressed in a red suit, surrounded by cameras and flashing lights. A familiar figure, yet something about him seemed different. His eyes, his smile, the way he seemed to be pulling the strings, almost as if he were orchestrating the entire event from the shadows.

It was Santa.

But it was more than that. Martin could feel it. This wasn't just a man in a suit. It was the demon himself, the one who had been controlling humanity's narrative for centuries. The time of revelation had come.

As he sat frozen, watching the broadcast, he felt a sudden surge of terror, as if the very air around him had shifted. He knew then that it was too late. The conspiracy he had uncovered wasn't something he could stop. It was far too entrenched, far too powerful. The world was already too far gone. He had been a fool to think that anyone would listen, that he could make a difference.

The whispers grew louder. The walls closed in on him, and he realized with horrifying clarity that he had become part of the plan. In his search for the truth, he had opened himself up to it. Like everyone else, he was a puppet. And now, there was no escape.

The final broadcast cut to black, and for a moment, there was only silence. Then, the familiar jolly laughter echoed through the room, filling his mind.

"Ho ho ho," Santa's voice boomed from the screen, but this time it was different. This time, it was an order.

Martin's mind screamed, but there was no escaping it.

The conspiracy was complete.

And he had become part of the lie.

146

Get Another Book Free

[1]

We love writing and have produced many books.

As a thank you for being one of our amazing readers, we'd like to offer you a free book.

To claim this limited-time offer, visit the site below and enter your name and email address.

You'll receive one of our great books directly to your email, completely free!

https://free.copypeople.com[2]

---

1. https://free.copypeople.com

2. **https://free.copypeople.com**

Did you love *The Christmas Deception Unmasking the Dark Truth of Santa*? Then you should read *Legends of the Damned: Villains Who Defied Fate and Conquered All*[3] by Morgan B. Blake!

In a world where darkness reigns and fate is merely a suggestion, these are the stories of the villains who shattered the chains of destiny and bent the world to their will. *Legends of the Damned* delves into the hearts of history's most feared antagonists—those whose evil transcends the ordinary, whose power reshapes reality itself. These are the tales of the Mirage Artist, who brings nightmares to life with the stroke of a brush, the Void Seeker, who feeds on despair and turns souls into hollow shells, and the Clockwork Tyrant, a master of machinery who commands an army of mechanical minions to crush entire cities.

---

3. https://books2read.com/u/mBRJwN

4. https://books2read.com/u/mBRJwN

Every villain here is more than a mere villain—they are gods of their own making, wielding forces too dark for mere mortals to understand. But with every victory, every conquest, comes the inevitable cost: the emptiness of their triumphs, the hollowed-out souls left in their wake. These legends are bound by the curse of their own power, each facing a twisted end where no one survives, not even them.

From the depths of forgotten dreams to the blood-soaked streets of decimated cities, this anthology uncovers the twisted, dark journeys of these villains who conquered everything... and yet lost it all. Prepare for a dark dive into their worlds, where no soul is spared, and where the final lesson is that even the most powerful of villains cannot escape the ruin they sow.

Are you ready to witness the ultimate fall from grace? Step into *Legends of the Damned*, where fate is not a prison—it is a weapon to be broken.

Also by Morgan B. Blake

The Hidden Truth
Silent Obsession

Standalone
Temporal Havoc
The AI Resurrection
99942 Apophis
The Shadows We Keep
Whispers of the Forgotten
Christmas Chronicles: Enchanted Stories for the Holiday Season
Realm of Enchantment Tales from the Mystic Lands
The Taniwha's Secret
Unicorn Magic Discovering the Wonders of a Hidden World
Vampire's Vow: Stories of Blood and Betrayal
Legends of the Damned: Villains Who Defied Fate and Conquered
All
Twisted Affection: How Love Can Break You
Lethal Beauty Inside the Minds of Women Who Kill
No One Left Behind Escaping the Shadow of War
The Spirit of Christmas: Heartwarming Stories of Holiday Magic
Forever Friends: Heartbreaking and Touching Dog Stories
The Christmas Deception Unmasking the Dark Truth of Santa